FOR RUXANDRA DRACULA

You called out to me; I heard you.
You spoke to me and I wrote,
My heart ached with your longing,
And we breathed as one.
When you cried, I felt your pain.
When you laughed, I felt your joy.
We completed this journey as one.
Daughter, I love you,
Just as if you were mine.
But instead, you are whole now,
And you no longer need me—
Be free, my child.
Be free.

Princess Dracula © 2017 by John Patrick Kennedy
Special thanks to Kindle Press for this amazing opportunity.
Cover art by Carlos Quevedo.

Interior layout and design by Colleen Sheehan

WWW.JOHNPATRICKKENNEDY.NET/

PRINCESS
DRACULA

JOHN PATRICK KENNEDY

2017

What is this world that is hastening me toward I know not what,
viewing me with contempt?

— *Khalil Gibran*

CHAPTER

ONE

JANUARY 1476
OUR LADY *of the* MOUNTAINS CONVENT,
near BUCHAREST

TOMORROW *I will be eighteen.*

Princess Ruxandra Dracula knelt in front of the cross in her initiate's cell. This was the last night she would spend in the small, plain, whitewashed room. The cold of the stones bit at her knees through her thick woolen skirt and cloak. Winter had enveloped the convent, and the cold had wrapped itself around all the buildings, leaving the nuns and initiates huddling together for warmth. With the window and shutters closed tight and the candle lit, the freezing air from outside still crept in, turning Ruxandra's breath into fog as she tried to call her mind to order.

She wanted nothing more than to be in her bed. Her bed warmer—a heated, towel-wrapped brick—was already spreading its warmth beneath the thick woolen blankets.

She shivered, then shook her head and closed her eyes. She had to pray before bed. It was her duty to pray.

Only, after tomorrow, it wouldn't be her duty anymore.

Her father, Lord Vlad Dracula, the prince—or *voivode*—of Wallachia was coming for her on her eighteenth birthday. He had sent word two months before.

Assuming he still lives.

He had been at war most of her life. Stories of victories and losses, of barbaric cruelty enacted on both sides, reached the convent on the mouths of merchants and townspeople. Most often, she heard of how nobly her father fought the war. But other times, less savory stories came. One which told of an entire town of men, women and children impaled by her father to stop the turks advance, gave her nightmares for weeks.

But according to the mother superior, he was coming tomorrow, and would take Ruxandra away to assume her rightful place at court.

But what is my rightful place? Will it be in his court? Or does he have someone he wants me to marry?

Perhaps she would be married to someone not too much older. Someone handsome and kind. Was there anyone like that among the aristocrats her father would choose from?

And perhaps her husband would allow her some freedom. She wouldn't be completely free, of course. That was impossible. But she had grown tired of the convent's rules. They made her wear a wimple to cover her long red hair, tied down so no one would see her breasts, and covered her head to foot. It was uncomfortable and Ruxandra would be glad to be done with it.

The bells rang. Ruxandra finished her prayers and rose. She blew out the candle, then climbed into the bed. The blankets brought warmth to her chilled flesh. She pulled them over her head, letting the heat embrace her entire body.

She was almost asleep when her door clicked open and two giggling, whispering shadows stepped in.

"Quick! Get inside," one girl hissed.

"I am," the other whispered.

"Shhh!"

Ruxandra pulled the blanket down just far enough to see the two girls shut the door behind them, stuff something under it to block any light, and throw a blanket over the shutters. A flint sparked one, twice, and a taper flared to life, lighting the faces of her friends.

Adela was a short blonde whose breasts pushed against her nightdress and were the despair of the nuns' attempts to instill modesty. Her parents had sent her to the convent in desperate hopes to keep her from scandal. And between her sweet, round face and her ability to lie shamelessly, she almost managed to make the nuns believe they were being successful. Valeria was slim and dark, a mischief-maker whose pranks had gotten her in trouble more than once.

They were both her lovers.

Adela called it practice for when they had husbands. Valeria called it wonderful. The nuns declared it a sin in no uncertain terms. And while Ruxandra did her best to obey the nuns in most matters, and to turn her thoughts to God and do his good work, she could not stop loving the girls. From the moment she'd first held Adela's hand, she'd known that, whatever else their feelings were for each other, they were too sweet to be sinful.

"What are you doing here?" Ruxandra whispered. "You'll get caught!"

"We had to come." Adela turned and applied the taper to the candle before it could burn her hand. "You're leaving tomorrow. We had to wish you happy birthday and say good-bye. You know the sisters wouldn't let us do that in the morning, so we're doing it now!"

"We brought treats." Valeria held up a small sack. "Raisin buns from the kitchen."

"And we brought extra blankets!" Adela threw them at Ruxandra. "So make room!"

The two girls piled onto the bed, almost crushing Ruxandra. They squeezed together, sitting side by side with their backs to the wall. Adela wrapped the extra blankets around their shoulders to ward off the cold of the stone behind them. Valeria rearranged Ruxandra's blankets, and the three let their legs tangle tight together. Valeria handed Ruxandra a small raisin bun. Ruxandra bit into it, savoring the sweet, rich taste of butter and herbs and juicy raisins. It was divine.

"I am so glad you're here," Ruxandra said around her bite of bun. "I was worried I wouldn't see you before I left."

"We would never allow that to happen." Adela kissed Ruxandra's cheek, letting her lips linger. "We're going to miss you, you know."

"Very much," said Valeria, putting her hand on Ruxandra's thigh.

A thrill ran up and down Ruxandra's spine.

"Plus we didn't want to neglect your education." Adela pulled out a small book with a plain, unmarked cover. "So we brought *this*."

Ruxandra peered at it. "What is it?"

"A gift from my fiancé." Adela grinned and opened the book.

Ruxandra's eyes went wide, and her cheeks flushed bright red. She clapped her hands over her mouth to stifle her laughter. "Oh my. Oh my God!"

The page showed a woman on her hands and knees, gazing over her shoulder at the man whose enormous penis was shoved deep into her sex. The opposite page showed a man on his back, the woman squatting over the top of an equally large penis, hand on the tip, ready to guide it inside her.

"I think he drew it himself," Adela said.

"They aren't that big," Valeria said.

"Horses aren't *that* big." Then Ruxandra's eyes grew wide. "Wait. How do *you* know?"

Valeria flushed. "Marin."

"Who delivers the vegetables? When? You never said!"

"Last week, after I helped him unload. He took me in the wagon." She pointed at the girl on her hands and knees. "That's how he started, but that's not where he finished."

"What?" Ruxandra's flush rose higher. "What do you mean?"

"Perhaps this?" Adela asked, turning the pages until she reached one with a woman on her knees, the man's sex in her mouth. Ruxandra's mouth fell open in shock. Adela turned some more pages. "Or this?"

The woman in the picture was bent over a barrel. The man stood behind her, his groin pressed against her backside.

"That," Valeria said. "I felt it for three days."

"At least you know you won't get pregnant." Adela poked Ruxandra's arm. "You should have done it with a man before you left, you know."

"I'm a princess. I must keep my virginity for my husband, unlike you little merchant girls." She wrapped her arms around both and squeezed them tight. "Besides, I *like* what we do together."

"So do I, but a girl needs variety." Adela turned the pages again. She landed on a picture of two women touching each other's bodies, their mouths wide and their tongues intertwined.

Valeria smiled at it and ran her hand higher up Ruxandra's thigh. "Now *that* looks familiar."

"Doesn't it though?" Adela cupped one of Ruxandra's breasts. "You didn't think we'd let you get away without saying a proper good-bye, did you?"

"Oh," Ruxandra gasped.

"Try to be quiet." Valeria turned the page. A woman lay on her back with her legs apart; a second woman knelt between her thighs, tongue on the other's sex. "Because I am going to try *that* on you."

Oh, God. Ruxandra felt heat rising in her belly as they took off her nightdress.

She barely managed to keep her gasps silent as their hands caressed her and they took turns kissing her mouth and neck and breasts. When Valeria knelt between her legs, Ruxandra grabbed Adela's hand and put it over her mouth to muffle her cries of passion.

The door slammed open.

"Filth!"

Sister Sofia, a candle in her hand and her eyes wide and blazing, glared at the three naked girls. "You dare profane the Lord's house with this obscenity! Shame! Shame on all three of you!"

"Please, Sister." Ruxandra sat up. She was the one leaving. If she could take the blame . . . "It was my fault. I seduced them. They were coming in to celebrate my birthday, and I—"

"Do you think me stupid?" Sister Sofia's harsh voice cracked like a whip. "I have seen the way you three look at one another, have watched you steal away from your chores to engage in your carnal pleasures."

"And you never joined us?" Adela rose, her large breasts jutting out toward the nun like a dare. "You should have."

Sister Sofia's slap *cracked* against Adela's face, knocking her over. The nun strode forward and grabbed the girl's hair, pulling her off the bed. "Be silent, you harlot! Ruxandra's final night at the convent should be a time of reflection and prayer. And by God, I will see that it is!

"You will all come with me now. And since you chose to be harlots, you can leave your clothing behind and show everyone your shame."

She forced Adela down into a half-crawl and dragged her from the room. Ruxandra and Valeria, naked and shivering, followed them down the hallway of the novice's building. Two other nuns stood by the outside door, disapproval clear on their faces.

Sister Sofia pointed at Valeria. "Open it. Now."

Valeria swallowed hard but did as she was told. A blast of wind blew snow into the building, driving pins of cold into their skin.

Sister Sofia dragged Adela into the freezing night. "Follow!"

The snow-covered stones burned Ruxandra's feet as she walked. The air sent chills through her naked body and numbed her skin. Her nipples were so hard they hurt. She thanked God for the high walls around the convent that kept the worst of the wind from them. Even so, it was horrible. Beside her, Valeria looked no less miserable.

Sister Sofia strode onward, ignoring Adela's swearing and cries of pain. She led them to the small penance chapel where those who had sinned prayed for forgiveness. Sister Sofia stopped in front of it and threw Adela to the ground. The girl whimpered.

"On your knees, slattern. Facing the chapel. You too, Valeria. Arms out."

Adela rose to her knees, extending her shivering arms like a martyr ready for crucifixion. Valeria knelt beside her. Sister Sofia grabbed Ruxandra's arm, marched her in front of them, and turned to face them. "Kneel. Arms out."

Ruxandra did. The other two nuns had followed and now took up positions behind her two shivering friends. As one of the nuns raised a pair of long straps, Ruxandra closed her eyes.

"I cannot punish you, *Princess*," Sister Sofia said, disgust dripping from the last word. "Not with your father coming tomorrow. But by God, I will punish your friends, and you will witness what your sins have wrought."

"Please, Sister," Ruxandra begged. "Please don't—"

Sister Sofia grabbed Ruxandra's hair and twisted it, making her cry out. "Begin the Prayer of Repentance. *Now.*"

Tears burned in Ruxandra's eyes. She blinked them away. She wouldn't cry. Not with her friends about to be beaten. Instead, she forced a deep, steadying breath and then began reciting. "O Lord, my God, I confess that I have sinned against you in thought, word, and deed."

The two nuns swung their straps, and the thick leather bit into the freezing flesh of Adela and Valeria's backs. Both girls screamed and convulsed.

Ruxandra forced her voice to stay steady. "I have also omitted to do what your holy law requires of me."

The straps swung again, and red droplets spattered against the snow beside Adela.

"But now with repentance and contrition, I turn again to your love and mercy."

Again more blood. More screams.

"I entreat you to forgive me all my transgressions and to cleanse me of all my sins."

The nuns swung the straps again.

"Lord, fill my heart with the light of your truth. Strengthen my will by your grace."

"Enough!" The mother superior's voice rang through the yard. She strode across the yard—a small, wizened woman who radiated power and strength. She pointed a finger at the two nuns with the straps. "You, get those girls to the infirmary at once."

"Mother." Sister Sofia stepped forward, her voice shrill. "These girls—"

"Are *my* responsibility." Mother Superior's tone brooked no argument, and she gave Sister Sofia a hard stare. "Go into the chapel. Pray for what you have done, and know that I will see you in the morning to discuss this matter at length. Princess, come with me."

Ruxandra pushed herself up, her knees frigid and aching from the freezing stones. She watched Adela and Valeria being dragged across the yard by the nuns. Neither looked at her. Ruxandra bit her lip and followed the mother superior into the chapter house. The warm air surrounded Ruxandra the moment she stepped in, making her freezing skin burn. A nun stood in the doorway, waiting.

Mother Superior nodded at her. "Take the princess to the kitchen. Clean and dress her."

The kitchen was warmer than the front hall. The nun wrapped Ruxandra in a blanket and made her sit at the table as she stoked the fire, put a large pot of water over it, then brought in a larger tub. Ruxandra pulled the blanket tighter around her body, wishing Adela and Valeria were with her.

The water took a long time to heat, longer still for the nun bathing Ruxandra to be satisfied with her appearance. By the time she was clean and dressed once more in the robes of an initiate, the bells for *Orthros*—morning prayers—rang out. The nun inspected Ruxandra once more, then led her to Mother Superior's office.

The mother surveyed her, nodded, and dismissed the other nun. "Your father will be coming for you soon."

"Yes, Mother." Ruxandra swallowed. "Please, Adela and Valeria—"

"Will spend the next two weeks eating a slice of bread a day and drinking only water. They will spend their time on their knees in the chapel in prayer, to think better on what has happened. You will not see them before you leave."

The mother superior rose from her seat. She was shorter than Ruxandra but had a presence that made the princess feel small.

"You are a child of the *voivode*. You have a duty—to your father, to your husband-to-be, to the people over whose lives you will rule—to be better. You must serve as a guide and inspiration and lead by example. When the nobility fails to judge the cost of their actions, people suffer. When *you*, Ruxandra, fail to judge your actions, others suffer."

Ruxandra nodded, unable to speak.

"Go to the penance chapel, my child, and pray until your father arrives. Pray that God gives you the strength to be a holy and just woman. Pray that you may help guide your future husband to better himself and the lot of your people. Go now."

The penance chapel was cold and dark. Ruxandra knelt on the floor, ignoring the bruises on her knees, and prayed, first for her friends to heal and suffer no more at the hands of Sister Sofia. Then she prayed for herself, that she not fall into temptation again and that she serve as a better example to all.

The door to the chapel opened, and a nun said, "Princess, Prince Dracula has come."

CHAPTER
TWO

L ORD VLAD DRACULA, *voivode* of Wallachia, was a tall man. His steel helmet shone bright in the morning light, as did the chains of his armor where they peeked through his thick red surcoat. His horse wore armor too, with thick pads to keep the cold of the metal from its skin. Mother Superior stood beside him, so small in comparison. Two dozen men on horseback sat at attention behind him. They were knights of renown. Ruxandra had been told in the letter her father had sent, they were men chosen for their skill and courage. They wore the same armor as her father, and most were young and handsome beneath their shining metal helmets. And yet Ruxandra could not take her eyes off Vlad Dracula.

Her father.

She had been eight the last time she'd seen him. For most of her childhood he'd been away at war, or in council, or supervising his sons' training for battle. He'd spent little time with his daughters. Zeleska, her sister, had been packed off to another family to be wedded to their son before Ruxandra left for the convent. But the few times Ruxandra remembered being with him, he had been kind. There had been sweets once and a small doll. And he'd always worn a thoughtful expression, as if he weren't quite sure what to make of her.

Now a thick beard hid most of his face, and the helmet covered the rest, save for the sharp glitter of intelligence in his brown eyes, the same rich chestnut as hers. He looked every inch the feared, terrible warrior of the stories. He looked her up and down.

Ruxandra curtsied low, her back straight and proud. "Father. Welcome."

Vlad's eyes bore into hers, but he said nothing. Instead, he turned to Mother Superior. "Have you followed all my instructions in regard to raising her?"

"We have. In every way." The Mother Superior spared a small smile for Ruxandra. "She has grown into a pious, proper young lady. She speaks Hungarian as fluently as she speaks our own language, and has some Italian and German. She knows proper household skills and—"

"Does she know how to ride?" Dracula interrupted.

The riding lessons had been a surprise to Ruxandra. Most ladies rode in carriages and wouldn't be seen on the back of a horse. Ruxandra loved it even if she'd only been allowed to ride around the inside of the convent once a month.

If the Mother Superior was offended by the interruption, she gave no sign. "She does."

Prince Dracula raised a hand, and one of his knights rode forward, leading a light brown palfrey with a sidesaddle. The knight dismounted, then knelt before her, his hands cupped together for her to step up. Ruxandra looked to her father, then to Mother Superior.

"Mount, child," the old woman said. "And think fondly of us in the years to come."

"Yes, Mother." Ruxandra stepped into the man's hands and let him raise her up to the saddle. With a few adjustments, she had her leg hooked around the saddle post and her cloak spread around her. "Please say good-bye to Adela and Valeria for me," she said as she pulled her hood up.

"Of course. And please, remember what I said last night. Pray, my child: for virtue, for strength, and for guidance."

"We ride," Vlad Dracula said. "Come."

The men turned their horses and then rode back out the gate. Prince Dracula followed them without looking back. Ruxandra stared in surprise. Her father had not said a single word to her.

"Go, child," Mother Superior said. "Quickly."

Ruxandra snapped the reins on the horse's neck. It trotted forward, catching up with the soldiers' heavier warhorses, with their burdens of armor and knights. She urged it faster until she rode just behind her father. She thought to call to him, but the man's straight back was as imposing as his horse and armor. It created a wall she didn't dare penetrate. So she rode in silence.

But that didn't stop her from looking at everything as they passed.

Ruxandra had not seen the world outside the convent gates since her eighth birthday, when her father brought her. It had been cold then, too. Staying at the convent seemed like a great adventure. No one had told her she would be there for ten years. But with the war and the pressure on her father to align himself for political gain, he had thought it safest to keep her there.

The trees here were no different than those on the convent grounds, the fields no less covered with snow. But each one she passed reminded her that she was entering a new world, a new life. She wondered if she would see her mother or if she would be taken straightaway to her husband or to her father's court.

The thought of her mother—tenderness, a hand on Ruxandra's cheek, soft gray eyes—made her heart ache. She pushed the memory away, like she had done a thousand times before. It had been difficult in the early years. Now it was second nature, much like the prayers and the hard discipline of mind and body the nuns had instilled in her.

Ruxandra's stomach made an alarming gurgling noise. She prayed no one else could hear it over the sound of the horses. She had not eaten since the raisin bun and wondered when the procession would stop to eat. Her father would not let her starve.

Would he?

They rode through the morning. The high road had been swept clear of snow by the wind, allowing them to make good time through the forests and fields. The last of the snow clouds had passed, leaving a clear blue sky above. Ruxandra delighted in the sun on her face and shoulders, even the winter sun. Most of her time in the convent had been spent indoors, studying, praying, and learning the womanly arts of sewing, needlepoint, and weaving. The riding lessons had been the wonderful exception.

When the sun reached its zenith, Prince Dracula barked an order. His knights reached into their coats and pulled out small loaves of bread, which they began to eat without slowing their pace. One of the men rode up beside Ruxandra and extended a loaf.

She took it and smiled. "I thank you, sir."

The knight nodded. He was handsome. He had a strong jaw with a tidy beard, and hazel eyes that had lingered on her before he rode away and resumed his place in the line. Perhaps he was a young lord, serving in the ranks of the *voivode's* army. Maybe he was even the young lord her father wanted her to marry.

She amused herself with the fantasy as they rode. The sun began descending in the sky, and Ruxandra grew cold. The air was still frosty, and her breath formed clouds that streamed past her. She supposed the men in their armor were much colder, but they were trained knights, inured to such discomforts. Even so, she wished they would stop at an inn or some other place of rest. She would prefer an inn. She'd never stayed in one before.

There might even be music!

They continued riding as the sun turned the sky red and gold with the promise of night soon to come. It grew darker, the riders in front of her became grey ghosts, barely visible in the dying light. At a barked command from her father, the men lit torches, sending a warm orange-yellow glow onto the snowy woods around them. The heat from the closest ones reached Ruxandra's face, providing some warmth in the cold dark. Her stomach rumbled again, but she said nothing. There had to be a reason they were riding so late into the night.

"Halt!" Her father's voice rang through the column of men. "Bring the princess forward!"

The handsome knight reached over and took the reins from her hands. He kicked his horse in the ribs then led Ruxandra through the ranks of men. Her father had already dismounted. The knight stopped his horse and hers a moment later.

Her father raised his eyes, made black by the dim light. "Dismount, daughter."

A knight went to one knee beside her horse; another offered her his hand. Ruxandra took it and swung down, lightly stepping on the kneeling knight's thigh before alighting on the ground.

Prince Dracula nodded his satisfaction. "Men, dismount and make camp. I will rejoin you in the morning. Daughter, this way."

Her father held out an arm for her to take and placed her hand in the crook of his elbow. He led her away from the camp and down a path just wide enough for the two of them to walk abreast. It had been cleared of snow, and the brush on all sides had been cut back. He led her—without looking at her—down a long slope to the bottom of a valley. She was desperate to ask where they were going but knew better than to say anything.

Trees surrounded them, making it impossible to see more than a few feet in either direction. Then the night was split by the orange glow of two torches planted in the earth on either side of a cave mouth. Prince Dracula took Ruxandra's hand off his arm, gripped it hard, and led her inside.

She expected the cave to be darker than the forest. Instead, candles had been placed along the narrow tunnel leading into the earth. She gripped her father's hand. Unable to keep silent longer, she said, "Father, where—"

"Be silent."

She closed her mouth.

The tunnel opened wide into a large chamber. Dozens of candles were placed along the walls, giving a bright yellow glow and heating the room. For the first time all day, Ruxandra felt warm. She pulled back her hood. *I am indeed on an adventure. If only Adela and Valeria—*

"Is this she, my lord?"

Ruxandra turned. There was another chamber, deeper than the one she stood in. Four men emerged. All were large, with armor on their bodies and swords at their sides. They examined her head to foot with their eyes—so much so that she began to blush. Then they turned back to Vlad Dracula.

He nodded. "Is everything prepared?"

"Yes, my lord," the tallest man said. "But will it work?"

"I do not know," Prince Dracula said. "The books say that it is a true ritual, but there are none alive who attempted it. I only know that we must take every chance, if we are to defeat the Turks."

The tall man looked at Ruxandra, something resembling pity in his eyes. "Even this?"

"Yes," Dracula's voice was cold and hard. "Even this."

He let go of Ruxandra's hand and he shoved her hard, propelling her into the four men. "Strip her."

Ruxandra couldn't understand what he was saying. It didn't make sense. Then the first man yanked her cloak over her head, leaving her caught in the dark material. One man grabbed her arm and shoved at it, trying to push it back inside the cloak. Ruxandra tried to pull away, but his grip was like iron. Another set of hands grabbed her from behind, shoving the cloak up her back. Someone rubbed a hand against her backside, making her scream.

This can't be happening! I am a princess!

She struggled, whipping her body, trying to kick at the men but unable to see anything. They were around her, quiet, save for the grunts of effort as they tried to tear away her clothing. Then the cloak slipped off, and she could see again.

Her father stood on the other side of the chamber, watching her with no expression.

Why? The tale of the villagers impaled to frighten the advancing Turks, leapt into her mind. *No! I am his daughter! He wouldn't!*

The man behind her caught both her arms and another grabbed her legs. The other two pulled out long, sharp daggers. Ruxandra screamed and tried to pull away as they began cutting away her dress and shift. Her legs were naked first, then her groin and backside. She struggled to cover her body, but the man behind her kept her hands pinned behind her back. The other two kept cutting, pulling away the last of the cloth, leaving her breasts bare for them all to see. She screamed, releasing her rage and helplessness.

Her father slapped her across the face, hard and fast and unforgiving. "I said be silent."

"Father, why—"

He slapped her again, hard enough to make her head spin. "Raise her."

The man behind him held her arms tight. The ones on either side grabbed a leg and pulled her feet from the ground. She screamed again and bucked her hips. The fourth man grabbed her around the waist to keep her still. The men on either side pulled her legs apart. Her father stepped forward.

"No. No, please, Father. Please," Ruxandra begged as he raised his hand. "Please, no. Please. What are you doing?"

"She is intact," Vlad Dracula said, his voice cold and hard. "Take her in."

The four dragged her into the other chamber. The light was dim, coming from the flickering flames of candles spaced out along the walls. A pentacle, twelve feet across, painted in red, took up the middle of the floor. At each point sat a human skull with an unlit black candle atop it. Ruxandra tried to understand what she was seeing but had no time. They shoved her onto the floor and pinned her arms and legs. One man grabbed something out of her sight, and a moment later cold metal clamped down on her wrist. The man on the other side did the same thing. Then all four worked to pin her legs to the ground and spread them wide so they could chain them too. She lay spread-eagle on her back. The ground was cold and hard, and the chains would not give, no matter how much she pulled on them. Her face grew hot with shame that overcame her fear. Her breasts, her legs, even her sex were on display for the five men in the room.

But none of them spared her a glance.

The four men each took place at a different point of the pentacle, outside the circle. Her father walked around it, lighting the black candles before taking a place at the top of the star, above Ruxandra's head.

"Father," Ruxandra begged. "Please, Father. What is happening? What are you doing to me? Have I offended you? Please!"

"Let us begin," Vlad said, not looking at her. He raised his left arm and took out a knife. With a single, swift cut he opened his palm. A moment later, blood dripped from his hand into the circle. The other four men did the same, and blood pooled in small puddles in front of each.

"Let the circle be sealed by our blood," Vlad said. "Let it be our bond and our protection, that the one we summon will hear our call and obey our demands."

"Let it be so," the other four said in unison.

"Let the girl be our sacrifice. Let her virginity be our offering. Let it appease the one who is to come," Vlad continued.

Again the other four spoke as one. "Let it be so."

"No!" Ruxandra thrashed on the floor, desperate to break the chains that held her. "Please, no! No! I don't want this! No!"

Her father's voice rose over hers. "Let the chant commence, and let us bend our will to the darkness that it may aid us in the days to come."

"Let it be so!"

Ruxandra screamed, long and loud, as the men chanted. The words were Latin and Greek and other, more guttural languages, all running together to make a deep and dirty sound, with a rhythm like a gravedigger's shovel scraping against rocky earth. The men kept their dripping hands held out, their eyes forward, and repeated the words over and over and over. Ruxandra's screams faded to tears and wails. No one would come to help her. No one would save her. She tried to pray, but fear jumbled the words into nonsense.

The five candles in the corners flared higher than should have been possible. All five men stared but did not stop chanting. The flames changed color from bright yellow to deep red, as if the blood on the floor had been turned into light. They flickered and danced, though there was no wind, and threw monstrous shadows over the walls of the cave. The room grew darker.

From the ground around Ruxandra came a thick, black smoke that stank of sulfur and rotten meat. It made her cough and choke. The lines of the pentacle began to glow the same deep red as the candles. The men's voices rose, higher and louder, and the chanting grew faster and faster. In the midst of it, her father's voice bellowed out.

"Dark One, I command thee! Come forth!"

A terrible noise, like stone tearing itself apart, echoed through the chamber and shook the cave walls. In the pentacle, inches above Ruxandra's body, a black hole appeared. It oozed darkness and drowned out the red light of the candles and glow from the pentacle. The air turned so cold that it froze and burned at once, leaving Ruxandra's flesh blistered.

Lightning, as black as the hole itself, spewed forth, bouncing off the ceiling and echoing around the chamber. The force of the thunder that followed sent the five men flying through the air to crash into the cavern walls. Thunder rolled through the room, shaking the ground hard enough that its convulsions slammed into Ruxandra's back, bruising and battering her. There was another clap of thunder and more black lightning that blinded Ruxandra with its blazing darkness.

And when she could see again, a tall, naked, black-winged woman stood above her.

The creature's white skin shone against the darkness. A waterfall of black hair fell from her head to her backside. Her breasts were large and as pale as the rest of her, with white nipples that pointed out hard, like diamonds. Her eyes glowed red, ringed with ebony lashes. Her mouth opened wide, revealing a row of long, pointed teeth. Her fingers ended in golden talons that looked capable of tearing a man's head off with a single swipe.

She was a nightmare of beauty and ferocity, with a perfection of feature and line not found on Earth. Ruxandra was stunned out of fear for a moment. That such a creature could exist—that the nuns' embroidered tales of demons, were not only true but were a bare and pathetic next to the real thing. This demon. This queen.

The creature looked around the room, her gaze cold and sinuous as a snake's. Then she gazed down at Ruxandra. Her fiery eyes pierced Ruxandra's skull. In an instant, Ruxandra knew that this creature could see her thoughts, unveil her secrets and memories. The eyes felt like a tongue, raspy and warm, licking the corners of her mind. Tremors shook her body, and more tears rolled down her face, though she couldn't make a sound. This ravishment didn't hurt, but it left her feeling more helpless than she had when the men were stripping and binding her.

The demon woman's eyes roamed over Ruxandra's naked flesh, lingered at her breasts and her sex. Then she raised them to the men around the room.

Her voice was soft and melodious and as cold as the darkness she had stepped from. "What mortal was so foolish as to summon me?"

THREE

R UXANDRA STARED UP at the demon, mesmerized. The creature looked back at her and smirked. "So you think I am beautiful, little sacrifice?"

"Dread demon!" Vlad Dracula pushed himself off the cave floor, then stood on shaky legs. "I have summoned you in accordance with the laws of heaven and hell, in ritual with blood and sacrifice. I have gathered men of stout heart and valor, and we have spoken the words of binding. You are in our control and powerless against what we have wrought."

The demon's left eyebrow rose, but she said nothing. Vlad took his place atop the pentacle. His men, still shaken from the force of the lightning, rose and staggered to their own places.

"Hear me, demon," Vlad said, voice booming. "Hear the bargain we will strike. See the sacrifice before you! We have need of power. Power to defeat the infidel who defiles Christian lands. Power to rule Wallachia and to protect it from those who would conquer it."

The demon knelt beside Ruxandra. "Did you know you were to be the sacrifice, girl? Did you come here of your own volition? Or were you dragged from your home and brought here against your will?"

"I—" Ruxandra couldn't speak. The long, sharp teeth of the demon's smile were far too close.

"Demon!" Vlad's voice rang through the chamber. "Do not seek to distract us! Nor to deceive us. You will do as you are bidden, and you will give what is asked. You will bestow us this power, and in return, you may take the virginity and life of that girl who lies before you."

"Oh, may I?" Sarcasm, thick and viscous, coated the words. The demon touched Ruxandra's face, letting her finger trace the line of her jaw. "You are pretty. And a virgin, he says. Only regarding men, I am guessing, from the smell on you."

Her eyes pierced Ruxandra's again, and memories welled to the surface of Ruxandra's mind. Her face turned red, and she tried to look away from the demon.

The demon cocked her head and smiled. "What sweet friends you have, little one. As to virgins, I prefer boys. There's nothing like the face of a young man when he realizes he won't be the one doing the penetrating."

The creature stood. Its flesh blurred and flowed, and from between its legs grew an enormous, erect phallus, bigger even than the ones in Adela's pictures. It pulsed, like a creature with its own mind, eager to begin driving into flesh. Ruxandra's eyes went wide with horror. The demon smiled. "They all scream, of course. Even the ones who like it."

Ruxandra began to cry again. The demon laughed. Her flesh blurred again, and the phallus vanished. "What infidels are these, Prince Dracula, that you would vanquish?"

"The Turks."

"And why should I grant you this power?"

"You have been summoned! You are here to do my will and bidding. It is my bidding that you make myself and these four men invincible in battle so that we may smite our enemies."

"You five?" The demon looked around the circle, taking in the others. "Five old soldiers. I think some more impressive physical specimens would have been appropriate."

Vlad's eyes flashed, and his next words came out through gritted teeth. "Each of these men is a leader in my army and a great warrior. Each will inspire his men to greater efforts through his invincibility. Now, take your sacrifice and grant my desire!"

"Or what?"

His face grew red. His next words came out in a snarl. "Or we will seal this cave, with you in it, in the circle, to stay here for a thousand years or more."

"Well, that would be unfortunate, wouldn't it?" The demon knelt between Ruxandra's legs and leaned over her. "Close your eyes, girl."

Ruxandra squeezed her eyes tight. She prayed that the thing would not tear her apart. *I don't want to die here. I want to live.*

The metal at her wrists and ankles ripped apart with a loud, fast screech. Ruxandra's eyes flew open in surprise. The demon wrapped its large hands around her shoulders and lifted her into a gentle embrace. Her flesh was hot and smelled of sulfur. Her breasts were soft and firm against Ruxandra's as she gathered the girl to her chest. One hand slipped underneath Ruxandra's backside. Then Ruxandra was lifted from the ground. In surprise, she wrapped her arms around the demon's neck. For a moment she felt reassured.

The demon rose to her feet, carrying Ruxandra as like a child. She smiled at Prince Dracula. "I think not."

"Demon, do as you are told! By the ritual and the blood, you were summoned," Vlad shouted, his face going deep red. "By sacrifice, you are controlled, and by the laws of heaven and hell you will obey me!"

The demon's smile grew wide, like a lion baring its fangs.

She turned a slow circle. "I can sense your lives, mortals. I know what disease will kill each of you, should you survive your battles. I know which of you prefer women and which prefer boys. I know what you ate for breakfast, and I know every sin you have committed since your birth, and you think *this*"—she gestured to the pentacle—"could control me? Fools."

"You will obey," Vlad said, his voice commanding and short. "You will give me power!"

"I will give you nothing," the demon hissed. She looked at Ruxandra. "What is your name, girl?"

Ruxandra thought she was too terrified to speak, but she managed to speak the words. "Princess Ruxandra Dracula, daughter of *Voivode* Dracula."

The demon looked back at Vlad. "You believe betraying your own flesh will give you more power?"

"I command—"

"Nothing!" The demon's voice shook the cave, louder than the thunder that accompanied her arrival. It took two steps outside the pentacle, facing Vlad, and pointed at the ground. "That thing is a toy, not a barrier. It does nothing but open the door, and nothing you can do will close it until I will it shut."

Vlad stumbled back, grabbing for his sword. The other four men drew their own weapons and ran to stand beside him.

"A company of fools," the demon said, surveying them, "too stupid to know they should not deal in powers beyond their world. Too stupid to realize that I and my kind are far, far more powerful than any human could even imagine."

Vlad pointed his sword at the demon. The blade shook. "This blade has been blessed and cleansed against such foul beings as you. I warn you, Demon—"

"*I am no demon!*" The words cracked like a whip. "I am one of those who fell with Lucifer. I am one who has lived in the tormenting fires of hell and will live there for all eternity. I have many, many men like you under my control there, and each one has broken, just as you will break."

She glanced at Ruxandra who remained limp and terrified in her arms. "He will kill you, girl. Do you want to die?"

Ruxandra couldn't comprehend the question. The fallen angel cared? She wanted her to live? That was impossible. No creature of hell cared for mortal life. The nuns who spoke of them made that clear. The fallen angels existed to torment the wicked and to ensure them an eternity of suffering for their sins.

"Decide now," the fallen angel said. "Do you want to die?"

Ruxandra shook her head.

The demon smiled. It wasn't a nice smile or a joyous one. It was a terrible, dark expression that spoke of horrors so deep as to be unfathomable. "Then you will not. Ever."

"What—"Vlad took a step forward. "What do you think you are doing?"

"Fifteen hundred years ago, my kind were banished, Ruxandra."The demon ran a gentle hand through her hair, like a mother petting a scared child. "We cannot roam the earth. We cannot dominate mankind any longer, nor make them bend to our will."

The demon lifted her hand to her mouth and ran the end of one finger over the tip of one of her teeth. The skin split open, and silver blood welled up on her fingertip. She lowered the finger to Ruxandra's lips. "Open your mouth."

Ruxandra wanted to protest, to beg for God's forgiveness and the creature's mercy, to run screaming from the cave, but she couldn't find words or strength in her limbs. She could do nothing but cry as the fallen angel parted her lips.

"I send you out instead, my child, " the fallen angel said, "to sow chaos and fear, to make humans kneel in terror and to ravage the world where I cannot."

"Stop!" Vlad's voice was shrill. "I command you to stop! Now!"

The fallen angel pushed open Ruxandra's mouth and slipped the finger inside. "Soon you will be freer than you have ever dreamed."

The drop of blood dripped from her finger onto Ruxandra's tongue.

Pain blossomed in her mouth like a flower of flame. It enveloped her head then her entire body. Every fiber of her being burned. Ruxandra opened her mouth and screamed, louder and longer than she ever had before.

Her body arched and convulsed. She was on the floor, though she didn't know how she'd gotten there. Her heels drummed hard against the ground, and her fingers clenched and unclenched of their own accord. Every inch of her flesh tore itself apart and rebuilt itself in a process that grew more agonizing with every moment.

"Shhh." The demon's voice penetrated her mind. "It will be over soon."

The world around Ruxandra was reduced to a blood-red haze. She could see nothing, and felt nothing except agony.

"I command you!" screamed Vlad Dracula though he seemed so far away. "By the laws of heaven and hell, I—"

"You do not know the laws of heaven or hell, human." The fallen angel's voice broke through the haze. "You want power? Here is power, embodied. Control her if you can."

Black lightning struck again, strong enough to break through the agony wrenching Ruxandra's body and mind. There was sudden cold, then heat, then darkness . . .

"Wake up!"

The words floated beyond reach, beyond sense. Ruxandra heard them but could make no sense of their meaning.

"Wake up!"

Something struck her face, the pain distant and sharp. She focused on it, focused on finding the source of the pain and the words and guiding herself out of the darkness toward them.

"Wake up, stupid child!"

Another sharp stinging pain hit her cheek, and this time, a small hole broke open in the darkness. The pain came again and again, and with each wave, she came closer to wakefulness. "Get up, you little whore!"

"She is useless," a second voice said. She still could not understand the words, but now she could hear them, and that was an improvement. The darkness around her paled to red. A third voice said, "We should leave her."

"She is my daughter. We can still marry her off," the first voice said, though the words held neither affection nor concern. She still could not make sense of them. Still could not understand anything except that her face hurt.

And that she was hungry.

Ruxandra opened her eyes. The cave, which she had vague memories of being dark and dim and red, seemed bright as day. The candles were like small shining stars, brilliant and bright and radiating their heat and light to strike every surface in the room. The walls of the cave were veined with different colors of rock, twisting and turning on themselves. Some shone white and pink. Others were a dull gray that sucked in the candle's gift of light. All of them emanated their own subtle light, making the room even brighter.

She wanted to look longer, but there was a man leaning over her. She *smelled* him—and four more like him nearby. She smelled their sweat, their fear. She smelled woodsmoke on their clothes, and the meat they had eaten, and the ale they had drunk for their last meal. She smelled the blood under the fingernails of one of them—another man's blood, not his own. And on and on—the world was a cacophony of scents . . . Here was a woman's scent, coming off the groin of one of the men, and there, a man's scent coming off another. One man had water on his boots, another had singed his cloak on the candle flames.

She could *feel* the blood racing through each man's body.

Their pulses beat like drums in her ears, calling to her, shaking the air with their strength. They sang to her and drew her like a moth to a candle's flame. Her mouth watered, and within, sharp teeth stretched from her gums. Her fingernails grew long and hard, like the talons of a hawk.

The man above her leaned in and grabbed her, pulling her upright. "Get on your feet, girl, or I'll beat you senseless!"

It took nothing to reach out and sink her claws into his neck. The armor on his neck resisted for a moment, then gave beneath the strength of her talons. The man shouted in surprise, then screamed in agony as the talons sank deeper and deeper. He punched at her face and tried to raise his sword. She felt the blows and saw the weapon but ir felt as though it was all happening to another instead of to her.

His pulse raced faster, the heat of his flesh burned against her fingers, and his blood flowed like silk over her skin. The delicious scents of copper and iron and humanity blended together in a single whiff. Her hunger reared, demanding she drink.

NOW!

"Stop!" Vlad Dracula, *voivode* of Wallachia, scourge of the faith and terror of the Turks screamed as his daughter's claws dug deeper into his flesh. "Please—"

She ripped Vlad's head from his neck, and his blood fountained out. Ruxandra buried her face in the gaping stump, her mouth wide, slurping and swallowing the hot, red life that sprayed from his body. The other men screamed in horror, then ran for their lives.

The blood gave warmth but no strength. The man was dead already, and eating the dead, she realized, did nothing for her. She dropped him and leapt across the room, blocking the men's escape. The man in front swung his sword, cutting deep into her side. Ruxandra ignored the wound. She lunged forward and sank her teeth into his throat. His shout of surprise turned into a gurgle. He spun and tried to shake her off, but she gripped him tight as she continued to drink.

It was so much better. It was not blood; it was life itself.

She relished in the life pulsing out of him and into her. It spread through her body like heat. She shuddered with pleasure, harder than she ever had with Adela and Valeria when their fingers touched and rubbed her to climax after climax. This was greater. Stronger. When his life faded from him, his knees buckled and he fell to the floor. The pleasure of it made her tremble from head to foot.

She needed more. Much, much more.

The other three men backed into a corner, their weapons in front of them and eyes wide with terror. One of them shouted something, but she couldn't understand the words. All she understood was his blood—precious, warm, life-filled and strong—calling to her.

She was across the room before he could raise his sword. Her teeth were in his throat before he could make a sound. She spun to put him between her and the other two, to keep their blades from biting into her as she drained his life in short, pleasure-filled gulps.

The next one died screaming.

The last one stumbled against the wall. He knelt to the ground and clasped his hands together. "O Lord my God, I confess that I have sinned against you in thought, word and deed. I have also omitted to do what your holy law requires of me. But now with repentance and contrition I turn again to your love and mercy. I entreat you to forgive me all my transgressions and to cleanse me—"

The words vanished in a gurgle as her teeth sank deep into his throat. He didn't struggle, didn't fight like the others. Whispered words slipped through his lips and to Ruxandra's ear.

"We brought this on our—"

The words were gone, and the last of his life faded away. Ruxandra dropped him, then scanned the room. There was nothing else to eat but she didn't mind. She was exhausted, like a man pushing himself away from the feast table, too full of food and drink to make sense. She stumbled back into the pentacle. The ground there was smoother than any other part of the room. Her eyes grew heavier. She lay down and closed her eyes, content in the smell of blood and death, warm and satiated from what she had drank.

As she tipped over the edge of consciousness, a single, coherent thought—her first since drinking the fallen angel's blood—slipped through her mind.

What have I done?

CHAPTER

FOUR

W HEN SHE AWOKE, the candles were gutted.

The scent of smoke still lingered, mixed with the tang of rock and dust and old, stale air. A subtle counterpoint to the overwhelming stench of blood and death that filled the cavern.

She opened her eyes and found herself staring at the walls of the cavern and then at the pentacle inscribed into the ground around her. The four chains the fallen angel had destroyed when she freed her lay in pieces around her.

A fallen angel. Among everything else—everything she was not yet thinking about—she felt awe.

It occurred to her she should not be able to see. She should be helpless in the darkness of the deep earth, reduced to crawling, hands outstretched, searching for a way out of the cavern. Instead, the cave was twilight dim. The rocks themselves glowed: lavender, pink, periwinkle blue. There was enough light to see the walls and the floor, the outline of the pentacle, and the jagged opening leading to the next cavern.

And the corpses.

Her father's head lay on its side in front of her. Sightless eyes stared at her, accusing. His mouth was wide open in a final silent scream. Below it, the bloody, shredded flesh of his neck hung red and dripping, with the white bone of his spine peeking through.

She screeched and scrambled backward out of the pentacle, moving until she hit the wall. Even then she kept pushing, pressing herself hard against the cave wall, trying to make her body meld with the stone and erase the horrors around her.

It wasn't possible. It *wasn't*.

She was just a girl. She couldn't kill five strong, armed, seasoned warriors. She couldn't have done that to her father. She didn't know how to fight, let alone kill. No human had the strength to do those things to another. She couldn't have stuck her fingernails into his neck.

But she remembered doing it.

Remembered sinking her talons into her father's throat and tearing until—

Her eyes darted to her hands. There were no talons, just fingernails, chipped and broken from where she had scraped them against the floor as she had struggled to escape the chains. She raised both her hands to her mouth, feeling over her teeth. There were no fangs; there was no way she could have bitten into anyone's throat. She couldn't have done it. It wasn't possible.

Something sticky covered her lips.

She rubbed at it and pulled her hands away. Something dark, congealed and clinging, covered them. It wasn't only on her hands either. It was on her breasts as well.

And her belly.

It had left streaks down her legs.

And matted the hair around her sex.

Her father's blood had coated her when she'd torn his head off and shoved her face into his fountaining neck.

Ruxandra Dracula screamed.

It was the sound of a feral animal, howling in pain and desperation. She didn't want to look at the bodies of the men she'd killed. Each time she turned her head she saw another, lying bent and still on the ground. On all the faces were expressions of terror.

She pressed her face to the wall and squeezed her eyes shut, but it didn't help. She could *feel* the men's flesh opening in her mouth, *taste* the hot blood pouring down her throat. She remembered her pleasure as she drank them, and it sickened her. She recalled the scents of the five men and how each one's blood tasted different and how each life felt different as it faded from existence. The last one had been the best, bright and steady and smooth as she drank.

She screamed again and again and again. When she could no longer scream, she prayed for deliverance. But God would not deliver her, she realized. He would look upon her and strike her down. She stopped praying and began to weep. She thought of Adela and Valeria, of her clean white bed in the small bare cell of the convent.

Where I had the audacity to be discontent.

Then Ruxandra, Princess Dracula, sobbed for her lost childhood.

When she was numb inside, she remembered her father telling his men that he would return in the morning.

They will find me. And they'll find the bodies, and they'll think I did it . . .

I did do it. She shuddered.

The fear of being discovered overrode the horror of what she had done. She pushed off the ground and rose to her feet. To her surprise, her legs didn't shake. She would leave. Maybe she could walk back to the convent. It had only been a day's ride, and the road was clear. All she had to do was get there. She would say . . . something. Anything. She picked her way through the puddles of blood and stepped over the bodies and went to the outer cavern.

Her clothes were destroyed.

Every piece had been cut open. The cloth stuck to the blood on her fingers. She picked up the remains of her shift and scrubbed at the blood on her hands and arms. It didn't want to come off, and she had to scrape at her skin. She dropped the shift and started to cry.

I have to get out of here. I must leave before they find me.

Her tears stopped. Anger flared at what her father and his soldiers had tried to do.

I will not take the blame for this.

She picked up the boots—they were intact, at least—then went back into the inner chamber. She looked over the four dead men on the floor, unable to bear looking at her father and his blood-covered corpse. The man nearest the door was closest to her size. He wasn't a light man, and the armor he wore beneath his cloak and surcoat meant that he would be even heavier and harder to move, but she needed to get clothes if she was going to walk back to the convent. She reached down and tugged on his cloak.

To her surprise, his body moved easily across the floor. To her even greater surprise, she was able to lift him.

There was some blood on the collar of the cloak but nothing compared to what covered her skin. She sat him up and stripped the cloak and surcoat off him like he was a sleeping child. She wrapped both garments around her body. It wasn't the same as the warm clothes she had before, but it would do. As an afterthought, she took his belt as well and wrapped it tight around her waist. Finally, she put on her own boots and left the cavern.

The light outside was as bright as day, and the air didn't feel as cold as it had the night before. Ruxandra started walking back along the path her father had led her down. Ahead, she could hear soldiers arguing.

"It's been a night and a day," one said. "He said he'd be back in the morning, and he has yet to return. None of them have."

Another, older voice said, "So whatever they are doing, they're still doing it. Or her."

One of the soldiers snorted. "That girl is a harlot? Looked like a novitiate to me."

"Thought it was his daughter," said another soldier.

"One of his by-blows more likely."

"Well, either way, he's not going to be sticking it in her."

"I don't know. You nobles are strange."

Laughter rippled through the company of men.

"Enough," snapped a voice. "He said he would be out in the morning. We must assume something is wrong, and must go look. I'll lead. Who is coming with?"

Three soldiers in turn said, "Me."

"Then let's go."

A torch flared to life then another. Ruxandra stepped into the shadow of the cavern. Then she realized it was the wrong thing to do. She'd been planning to sneak up to the camp, find the road, and follow the horses' tracks back to the convent. But with the men coming toward her, there was no way she could take the path back. She stepped off the path and into the forest. The brush swished around her, sending snow scattering. She began running. The snow wasn't deep, and she could move well enough, but it made noise. She dared a glance over her shoulder. The men's torches were little sparks of light, twinkling through the trees.

Ruxandra stopped, confused.

She could hear the men walking on the hard snow of the path, and the others talking and grumbling around the fire. She spotted them through the trees, and could see the bright steel of their helmets reflecting the torchlight, and their breath coming out in small frosted puffs.

She was seeing and hearing them as if they were 10 feet away, though they were easily fifty times that

And why do they have torches in the daytime? She glanced skyward.

The sky was clear and bright and the sun was nowhere to be seen. A thousand stars shone upon her, lighting the world as bright as daylight ever had.

What... how?

She took a deep breath to calm herself. Then another. Then she noticed that, when she breathed out, she could not see it. In this cold, her breath should have been an icy fog in front of her, but there was nothing. She took another breath and blew it out harder. Then another. Still no fog.

Do not think about it. Not now.

It wouldn't be long before the men reached the cave. When that happened, she had to be far away. If they caught her—

Get away first. Get away and find the road and think about it all later.

She began walking, ducking under branches and trying not to shake the snow off them. She listened as she walked, waiting for the men to shout for reinforcements. No sound came. She turned in the direction she thought the road might be and kept going. She could find it soon enough, she was sure.

Then I can return to the convent. Once I tell Mother Superior, I am sure they'll take me in. And maybe they can bless me and take away the sins of what I've done.

What my father did.

The thoughts went round and round in her mind, though she knew there was no answer to be found or one she could accept.

He did it because he could.

Because I did not matter.

She thought of the fallen angel's scorn—and kindness. Could a fallen angel care more about her than her own father? Yet what kind of care was it to make Ruxandra commit such crimes?

Well, she was a fallen angel.

My father didn't know what he was doing summoning her. Fool, she thought.

Hours later, she had yet to find the road or anything at all.

Lost. I'm lost.

The fear she'd managed to suppress started welling up. She moved faster and faster until she was running through the trees, knocking down snow and cracking branches.

I should have followed the guards. I should have stayed close, not gone in the opposite direction. I don't even know where I am.

Think, Ruxandra.

A valley. The cave was in a valley. She looked for any sign the ground was rising. *I've been running the length of it instead of going up.*

The ground to her left seemed higher. She turned, then ran harder. The woods passed by in a blur. The ground rose and fell then rose and rose and rose until she was sure she was out of the valley. She roused a burst of speed and broke through the woods into a clearing.

She skidded, trying to stop, and plowed to a halt halfway across the clearing. She looked back in surprise. The marks stretched back thirty yards.

How fast was I going that I would do that?

She tried to calculate it but couldn't. She had to have been moving very, very fast. Faster than anyone had ever run. Faster than a horse.

It isn't possible. None of it.

And yet I am doing it.

And I'm still lost.

She had hoped the clearing meant she was near the road, but there was no sign of it. No sign of anything except the gray and brown branches of the trees, interspersed with the green spikes of the evergreens. She turned in a slow circle. There was no sign of people—no buildings, no smoke rising, no paths through the forest or stumps marking a woodcutter's work. As near as she could tell, she was alone in the world.

The sky was growing lighter. The dark firmament with its many bright stars was giving way to the deep blue of predawn. Soon the sun would be visible, and the snow would be even brighter, and she would be better able to see where she was going.

Perhaps then there will be people out. Perhaps I cannot see anything because it's night, but when the sun is up, I'll be able to see the smoke and hear anyone nearby.

She looked for a place to sit and found a log that wasn't too covered in snow. She dusted it off the best she could then sat.

At least I don't feel cold.

I should be cold.

It was one of those things that, like many others, she decided not to think about. She wrapped her arms around her body and waited.

I wonder what Adela and Valeria are doing right now.

Praying, most likely. Ruxandra hoped Sister Sofia was doing far worse penance. Preferably something involving the pigs.

Cleaning the pans, she decided, on her hands and knees with nothing to use save her bare hands. It was a silly fantasy, Ruxandra knew, but it passed the time, and kept her from thinking of what had been done to her.

How could he have done that? My own father.

She turned her mind away from it and turned her eyes to the sky. She could see sun beams, peeking through the trees.

It was bright enough to hurt her eyes.

She watched as the sunshine slipped through the branches and crept its way across the ground. She had to squint, it was so bright. The closer it came to her perch, the warmer she grew until she felt like taking off the cloak. She should have been freezing, not hot. But as the light came closer, she felt like she did on a summer's day when the nuns excoriated the novitiates for removing their wimples to cool off.

Her eyes began hurting, almost as if she was staring into the sun, instead of watching the light dance among the woods.

Ruxandra closed them, letting her body bathe in the warmth. The sun would touch her soon, and then the long night would be over. And with luck, she would be able to find her way out of the woods and back to the convent.

And then?

I'll tell them something.

The sun crept over the snow and touched the toe of her boot. Ruxandra hissed and pulled her foot back. The touch of the sun had burned, right through the leather. The surprise brought her to her feet. Sunbeams pierced the trees and branches and landed on the bare skin of her face.

Then she was on fire and screaming.

CHAPTER
FIVE

R UXANDRA'S FLESH BURNED as if she had shoved her face into fireplace coals. Her hair burst into flame, and her skin erupted into blisters that burst moments later, exposing the charred flesh underneath.

The agony was terrible.

She screamed and hurled herself backward, falling over the log. Ruxandra pushed her face into the snow, rubbing it back and forth to cool her cheeks. She slapped hard at her head. The flames burned into the flesh of her palms. She pressed her hands into the snow, dousing the flames and dulling the pain.

When the sun touched the bare flesh of her calf, new agony erupted. She screamed again and stumbled to her feet. She ran, limping and crying. Sunlight glinted off the ice-coated trees and reflected off the snow. The reflected light hurt her eyes, made her skin heat up, but it was nothing compared to the unbearable agony of the sun's direct touch. She ran on and on, looking for shelter— any shelter. The sun rose higher, lighting the sky and the earth, threatening to burn her to a cinder.

She spotted a small gully and threw herself into it. There was an overhang on one side. The earth under it had been washed away, leaving a shallow hollow in the side of the gully. She crawled into the deep shadows under it. She squirmed and dragged and pulled until her entire body was in shadow. Her face and calf burned as if the heat were still on her. Tears streaked her face, and cries of pain that she couldn't control slipped out between her clenched teeth.

Outside, the sun crept forward.

Her eyes watered as she watched it inching across the landscape. It hurt to look, but she couldn't take her eyes off it. It was her death she watched. If the light touched her . . .

For hours she lay there, her body pressed tight against the back of the overhang, her face and hands and leg all burned in pain as the sunlight crept its way across the ground. She watched the edge of the light roll down the side of the gully until it touched bottom. She was on the wrong side, she realized. When the sun began to descend, it would reach into her little space and burn her alive.

The light slid across the gully floor, slow and unstoppable. And even though it hurt to look, Ruxandra could not take her eyes off the light. The way it glinted off the snow crystals, reshaping them as it went, fascinated her.

It was then she realized she could see the shape of each crystal on the gully floor.

There were thousands of them, and no two matched. They splayed out in spikes and squares and even triangles. And when the sun touched them, they re-shaped themselves, flowing and changing in the warmth of the light. Ruxandra watched them change, fascinated by how well she could see, almost to the point of forgetting her danger.

Sometime in the morning, Ruxandra's burns began to heal. They still hurt, but it had become the dull, throbbing pain of flesh repairing itself. And they itched, like ants crawling under her skin. She scratched and opened the healing flesh, bringing new pain.

She turned her eyes back to the snow, watching the crystals.

Then the sun started sliding down the far side of the sky, and the light began creeping under her overhang.

Ruxandra pulled her body as far back from the sun as possible. She wished she were willowy like Valeria and that she were back in the convent. She wished she were kneeling naked in the convent courtyard with the strap coming down on her naked flesh. But there was no escape for her. All she could do was watch as her death crept closer and closer.

I am going to go to hell. I am a murderer and a monster and I will burn in the lake of fire for eternity.

Will father be there, burning beside me?

The light vanished.

Ruxandra stared at the darkened ground. The sunlight was gone, though it was still daylight outside. She leaned forward, squinting out at the brightness. The sun had sunk below the tree line, cutting off the line of light that had threatened to end her life. She giggled, then laughed, howling with joy and relief. She had lived!

Somewhere in the midst of it all, the howls of laughter turned to sobs that shook her body so hard they threatened to send her tumbling back out into the daylight.

She would stay alive for another night.

And then what?

She was still lost in the woods in winter. She was still a murderer. And though she didn't have fangs and talons right then, she was no longer normal. She heard too well, saw too well, smelled too well. When the sun touched her, she burst into flame.

She had become a creature of darkness.

The thought brought more fear, and worse, an enormous loneliness. One of the nuns had once said that being damned meant being cut off from the divine presence. She had never dwelled on hell's grislier punishments like the other nuns did. She would only say, "None of us on earth—not even the worst sinner—can comprehend that unending apartness."

Ruxandra thought now she could.

At some point, in the midst of her tears and terrified thoughts, she fell asleep.

She awoke to howling.

Ruxandra's eyes snapped open. She cocked her head, listening. She couldn't judge how far away it was. But whether it was close or not, she knew she couldn't stay where she was.

She crawled out of the hole. The cloak and surcoat, already filthy with blood, were now caked with a layer of dirt, both inside and out. She was filthy and smelled of death. If the wolves got a whiff of her, they would chase her down.

The howls came again, long, deep, and soul-chilling. She crawled out of the gully and struck out in the opposite direction of the wolves. To her relief, the snow was not deep beneath the trees, and she was able to move at speed. The howling faded far behind her as she walked through the night. The other sounds of the forest filled her ears—small creatures moving beneath the snow, the wind shaking empty branches, the winter birds twittering in their nests. The air was clear and cold, though not so cold as to freeze her, which was a blessing. The snow had an aroma too, like the smell of rain but sharper and harder. Once, she caught the scent of something alive. It was a deep, musky smell, not like any animal she'd smelled before. With it came a deep rumbling snore, somewhere in the earth. She quickened her pace until she'd left it behind.

Smoke filled her nose.

Ruxandra froze. The smell was faint, almost imperceptible. She turned in a circle, sniffing the air. She walked a few paces, lost the scent, changed direction and found it again. She began running through the forest. Her feet moved unerringly, as if her body could sense the obstacles and avoid them. Then she reached the forest's edge.

She stood on the edge of a field, near a cluster of houses and barns surrounding a fortified manor house. The solid stone house had no windows on the ground level and slits for archers on the second. A stream of smoke came from the chimney, which carried the aroma of burning wood and something cooking.

Chicken broth, I think. They must be making stock.

She was surprised her mouth didn't start watering at the thought of it.

She strode between the houses to the manor, and pounded on the big iron door, hoping the noise would get through. No one answered. She pounded again, this time hard enough to rattle it on its hinges.

"Who the hell is knocking this time of night?" yelled a deep voice from the narrow slit above.

Ruxandra stepped back so the man could see her. "Please, let me in."

"Let you in?" the man echoed. "Who the hell are you?"

She pushed the hood of her cloak back and looked up at him. "Please, I am Ruxandra Dracula, daughter of Vlad Dracula, *voivode*—"

"By God's balls!" The man disappeared from the slit, and shouting came from inside. The man hollered at people to wake up and to rise and help.

"Get that goddamn door open! Now!"

The bar was taken from the door, and bolts were thrown back. A tall, older woman in a luxurious fur cloak pushed the door open, a lantern in her hand. She raised it high. "I am Lady Demetra. You are welcome, Princess Dracula."

All at once, Ruxandra began crying. The woman handed her lantern to a guard and pulled Ruxandra into an embrace. Ruxandra buried her face into the woman's shoulder. It was a relief, after days alone in the snow, to feel another person's warmth. And the longer Ruxandra held on, the more she could feel. The woman's heartbeat pulsed strong and steady in her chest, the force of it vibrating through her body as it sent her blood rushing through her veins.

Ruxandra was very, very hungry.

She pulled her away and stepped back. "Thank you."

"Of course." Lady Demetra took her hand. "This way, my child."

She led Ruxandra out of the small, stone entry room with its slits in the walls on both sides and hole in the ceiling for attacking anyone who tried to force their way in. They went through the great hall, whose walls were hung with tapestries and empty torch holders.

"Come to the kitchen, and we'll get you cleaned up," Lady Demetra said. "You're covered in dirt."

"Worse," Ruxandra said. She wiped at her eyes and tried to swallow back the sob that came with it. "Under the cloak and the surcoat. I am . . . they . . ."

"Shush, child," the woman said. "We can get you a tub if need be. Come to the kitchen. Then you can tell me what happened."

No, I cannot. But what will I tell them?

The woman led Ruxandra downstairs into the kitchen. It was warm with the glowing coals of the fireplace and smelled wonderful. There had been beef a short time before and pork and chicken over the past few days. There was a large pot of broth simmering over the coals. Two other women—one younger, one much older—were setting up the fire.

"Now come, child," said Lady Demetra, "give me your cloak."

Ruxandra hesitated, then undid the belt at her waist and let the cloak fall open. The women gasped at the surcoat underneath. "Dear God, child, is that all you've got on?"

"They cut my clothes off," Ruxandra said. "Just before they—"

She couldn't say what they had really done, so she let them believe the obvious instead.

"There's blood all over your legs," the younger woman said. "Are you hurt?"

"It isn't mine. There was a fight. People were killed. My father—" *I ripped his head off and drank his blood.* "My father was beheaded right beside me."

The young one's hand went to her mouth as if doing so would stop the horror. The older one shook her head.

"We heard of Prince Dracula's death," Lady Demetra said. "And we had heard his daughter disappeared as well. We thought . . . well . . ."

Ruxandra swallowed hard. "After the fight, I took these clothes from one of the dead men and ran into the woods. I've been lost ever since."

"You're lucky you still have all your fingers," said the old one. "It's a deep frost out there. Cold enough to freeze a body solid."

"Very lucky," said Lady Demetra. She picked up a bowl and began filling it with broth. "Gerta, heat water. Lusa, get the tub."

The older woman went off to the corner where a large wooden tub sat. The younger ran to a barrel and dipped a large pot in it.

"Take this," Lady Demetra said. "You must be starving."

Ruxandra took the bowl and sniffed. It was full of winter vegetables and herbs that had blended together with chicken fat and the juice of the meat. Ruxandra blew on it while the woman fetched a spoon. The first mouthful was an explosion of warmth and flavor. Ruxandra could taste each of the ingredients that went into it, and each one was wonderful. She savored each mouthful, letting the heat from the broth warm her from the inside out.

It was delicious. And it did nothing to fill up the hollow inside her.

The women took turns sitting beside her while the water for her tub heated. Each heartbeat filled her ears. The young one held her hand for a little while, and Roxanne felt the girl's pulse rushing through her skin.

It would be so easy to. . .

No. This time, I have a choice.

The water was finished, and the washtub set out in front of the fire. Lady Demetra helped her take off the surcoat, and all three women stared in horror at the dried blood on her. They poured water over her and started working.

Twice Lady Demetra made Ruxandra step out of the tub so Lusa and Gerta could throw out the bloody water. Each time the other two went past with it, the blood filled Ruxandra's nostrils, making her drool. She wiped a hand across her mouth, to make sure there were no fangs growing and to catch any spit.

Gerta fetched a dress—old and patched but clean and still serviceable. It was short on Ruxandra but covered her and didn't smell of blood or dirt and was so much better than the feel of the filthy clothes against her skin.

"There you are," Lady Demetra said. "Much better. Now, we must find you a place to sleep that's out of the way."

"My room," Gerta said. She blushed the moment it left her mouth. "I mean, it's really just a corner of the pantry, but it's warm and I'll not be using it during the day. Would that be acceptable, Princess? Until we find you better?"

Ruxandra nodded. "Yes. Thank you."

Gerta led her in and then helped her lie down. After the night in the dirt in the forest, the rough cloth of the blankets and the thick straw of the mattress felt wonderful. Ruxandra thanked the girl and closed her eyes. Hunger gnawed at her. Ruxandra pretended she was in bed back at the convent, sent there without supper for some misbehavior or other that she and Adela and Valeria would laugh at with the sunrise.

I'm not hungry at all. I don't need to eat. I'll be fine.

When she awoke, she was starving.

She crawled out of the bed and into the kitchen. It was empty, save for the old woman, Lusa, who sat on a short stool in front of the fireplace, her back to Ruxandra. Despite her age, her heart moved in a strong, steady rhythm, driving the blood through her veins with the vigor of one much younger. It called to Ruxandra, like a wounded animal cries called to wolves.

Her eyes locked on the old woman's neck. She took a step, then another, and before she knew it, she was behind the old woman. Lusa poked at the coals and sighed. She rose from the stool and stretched her back with a groan and a creak of old bones. Her heart sped with the motion, rushing to send blood to fill her moving joints as she stood and turned.

"Oh!" Lusa jumped back and stumbled. Ruxandra caught her with one arm to keep her from tumbling into the coals. Lusa gasped with relief. "You startled me, child."

Lusa's pulse rushed underneath Ruxandra's fingertips. The smell of the old woman—sweat and cooking grease and wood-smoke—filled her nostrils. Ruxandra's eyes dropped to the vein in Lusa's throat, watching it pulse in time with her heartbeat. Almost against her will, Ruxandra moved her face closer and closer to Lusa's.

"You've slept the day through," the old woman said. "Not surprising, with what those soldiers did to you. Come here, girl." Lusa pulled Ruxandra into her embrace. Ruxandra couldn't resist her. Her arms went around Lusa, and she rested her head on the woman's shoulder. Her mouth felt strange, different, and Ruxandra knew the fangs were back. Lusa hugged her tighter. "You'll be better soon."

No. Get away from me. I'll hurt you.

Her mouth opened, but no words came out.

Instead, Ruxandra turned her head sideways, drove her teeth into the old woman's neck, and drank.

CHAPTER
SIX

LUSA DIDN'T HAVE time to scream.

She pushed and fought, striking at Ruxandra with hands made hard and strong by years of working in the kitchens. She clawed at Ruxandra's face, trying to reach her eyes. Ruxandra closed them tight, crushing the woman to her body. Lusa's ribs creaked, and the air whooshed from her lungs.

Ruxandra *wanted* to stop. She tried to let go, tried to pull away from Lusa's body. She couldn't. Lusa's blood rushed down her throat. It filled her body with warmth and strength. Ruxandra wanted—*needed*—every drop of it.

Lusa's arms fell to her sides. Her struggles turned to spasms. Ruxandra felt the last of the old woman's life fading away, felt her soul leaving her body. Then Lusa was still. Ruxandra stopped squeezing, and the woman slid to the floor.

Ruxandra licked her lips to catch the last of the blood. Her fangs retreated into her gums with a *squish*. Ruxandra shuddered from the strange feeling. She gazed at her hands and saw that the veins were protruding, the old woman's blood turning them black as it spread through her body. She held them up, watching in horrified fascination as the black faded and her hands were once more pale and smooth.

She dropped them to her sides, and her eyes fell on Lusa's crumpled corpse. The old woman's eyes were opened. The holes in her neck did not drip, and her skin had gone pale and sallow in death.

Oh dear God. Ruxandra's knees trembled and threatened to give way. *What have I done?*

In the cavern, Ruxandra had acted on instinct. She had been a beast, unthinking, uncaring about anything except feeding. Though she remembered every detail, she'd felt nothing when she killed those five men. Nothing but hunger and relief as the blood flowed through her body.

This time, Ruxandra had known what she was doing . Even though she had been horrified, she hadn't been able to stop herself. She had realized what she was going to do as soon as she felt Lusa's pulse from across the room.

Worse, she had reveled in it.

I'm a monster.

I must leave before they discover the body. I must—

What?

What can I do? Where can I go?

The terrified stare on Lusa's face seemed accusatory. Ruxandra's hand went to her mouth again, as if she could wipe away the blood she knew wasn't there.

If I am around people, I'll do this again. And I cannot do this again. I will not. I must leave.

They had taken Ruxandra's surcoat, cloak, and boots. She had no idea how to get them back or if she could. The blood on the surcoat had been thick enough that it should have been destroyed, but the cloak might still be around. She just needed to find it and her boots. Then she could run. She wasn't sure where she would go or what she would do.

She stared down at the old woman's body. Tears blurred her vision. She reached down, hesitated, then knelt beside her. She wanted to close the old woman's eyes. She wanted to straighten her out. But she couldn't bring herself to touch the corpse. She began to cry.

"Lusa!" The voice was rough and male and strong and came from the stairs above. "Is there any tea left? I can't sleep. Lusa?"

Footsteps, heavy and hard, hit the stairs. Ruxandra stood up. Her throat closed with fear and grief, robbing her of words. She stood speechless and helpless when the big man stepped off the last stair and into the kitchen.

"Oh, the girl. You're awake then. Slept the day through, you—" He stopped, his eyes going wide. "Lusa!"

He ran forward, shoving Ruxandra aside. He knelt beside the old woman, then took her in his arms. "Lusa! Lusa! No—"

His body shook as he sobbed. He cradled the old woman in his arms. Ruxandra began backing away, her eyes never leaving him.

If I can reach the stairs, I can get out.

"What happened?" the man barked, causing Ruxandra to freeze. Grief made the words come out harsh. "Why didn't you call for help? Why were you just standing there?"

His face folded in on itself, and fresh tears began. "She was my nursemaid, you know. She looked after me as a wee one. God, she had a hard hand. Would whack me right upside the head when she was mad. Left my ears ringing."

He laid her on the stone floor. Ruxandra started backing toward the stairs again. She wanted to run away but couldn't take her eyes off him. He straightened the old woman's legs and then her dress. He crossed her arms, then turned her head to face up.

He saw the holes in her neck.

His body stiffened, and his eyes went wide. Even though Ruxandra knew she should run, she couldn't. She watched in dread and terrible pity as his trembling fingers traced over the two ragged holes. Confusion filled his face first, as if he couldn't understand what he saw.

His gaze rose from the old woman, locking on to Ruxandra. "What happened?"

Ruxandra couldn't say a word, couldn't do anything but stare at him.

The last of the grief faded from his face, replaced by bright red anger. His voice hardened, and the next words snapped out like Sister Sofia's commands. "What did you do?"

All Ruxandra could do was stare and tremble. Tears flowed down her face. The man rose. His legs stayed bent, like an animal ready to pounce. His hands curled into fists. "Answer me!"

Ruxandra searched for words, for excuses, but she could think of nothing to say.

"Answer me!"

Ruxandra's words came out soft and broken, like a child begging forgiveness for something she knows cannot be fixed. "I'm sorry. I'm so sorry."

He launched at her from across the room, his hands clenching her dress as he slammed her against the wall. *What have you done?*

"I didn't mean to!" Even as the words came out, Ruxandra knew they were a lie. "Please, I didn't want to."

"You killed her." His words were sharp, angry hisses. "You bit her and drank her and killed her, you demon."

"Please, no—"

"Demon!" The man's voice rose loud enough to reach the entire house. "Demon! Vampire! Murderer! Help! Murderer!"

"No!" Ruxandra shoved him hard. The fabric of the dress tore in his grip, and the man went flying backward across the room.

He yelled in pain as he hit the side of the fireplace. Ruxandra ran up the stairs and into the great hall. A babble of confused voices came from all around the house. Men in hard boots and armor ran down the stairs as women roused and called to one another.

From the kitchen, his voice filled with pain, the man still shouted. "Help! Murderer! Help!"

The inner doors were shut and barred. Ruxandra rushed to them and threw the bar off. It flew across the room, slamming hard against the wall. She hauled the door open and then ran to the outer doors.

"Stop right there!" a soldier shouted.

She spun, her back against the door. Three men had swords pointing at her. They appeared grim and angry and more than ready to kill her. She held out her hands. "Please. Please just let me go. Please."

"Stay right there until the lord comes," growled the oldest of the three. "And do not move one bit."

"Oh, God, please. Please. Just let me go."

"God?" The man from the kitchen appeared in the doorway. He held up a lit torch. The flames glowed red and yellow. "A creature like you shouldn't dare talk about God."

"What is going on here?" Lady Demetra demanded. She stepped into view, a night robe wrapped tight around her body. "Husband?"

"She killed Lusa." He pointed at Ruxandra, his arm shaking with rage. "She drank her blood and killed her!"

"What?" Lady Demetra's eyes went wide. Her gaze went back and forth between Ruxandra's torn dress and thin form and the fury on her husband's face. "How?"

"She's a demon." Her husband raised the torch. "She's a demon, and she needs to be killed right *now!*"

He stepped forward and shoved the burning wood at Ruxandra's face. She sprang back, her head banging against the door. He swung again. "Kill her!"

Ruxandra ducked the flaming torch. It hit the door, sending up a shower of sparks. She dodged one of the men's swords as he thrust at her stomach. A second man raised his arm to swing. Ruxandra screamed and turned. She slammed both hands against the door. The doors shuddered, and the bar holding them closed broke in two with a sharp *crack*. The doors swung wide open. Ruxandra almost froze in surprise, but she smelled the bloodlust of the men around her, felt the air moving as they raised their weapons.

She ran into the night.

The guards and the man howled in rage and followed, boots thudding on the frozen ground. She tore across the fields, leaving the men behind. Then she was in the woods, dodging through the trees and jumping fallen branches. The old woman's blood sang through her veins, filling them with a deep thrumming power. She ran far and long until there were no sounds of pursuit, only the night animals and the cold wind whistling through the trees.

She collapsed into the snow and wept.

Grief poured out of her. For Lusa, who had left an imprint on her mind of hard-won wisdom and iron strength. For her father and his men and what she'd done to them. Most of all, she wept for herself and what she had become. She had thought she could go back to the convent, that she could be safe there. But if she went back, she would endanger them all. She would not be able to resist the hunger, and when it came, what would she do?

A vision leapt into her mind: Valeria and Adela, their naked bodies entwined with hers, their eyes wide and staring, their faces twisted with horror as Ruxandra drained the blood from them.

"No!" Her voice rang through the forest, sending the night birds flying and causing rustles as the winter foxes dashed away into the darkness. She put her hands over her mouth. *I can't let them find me. They'll kill me. Or I'll have to kill them.*

The sky above started to lighten.

I'll have to kill myself first.

Suicide was against God's law. To kill oneself was to throw away God's gift of life, and that was the ultimate sin. *But I am not one of God's creatures anymore. I'm Lucifer's, made by one of his angels, for the purpose of destroying life. Surely, God will grant me mercy for stopping myself from killing again.*

Surely.

There was no question she was a monster. No question she should not be allowed to walk on God's Earth. She had hoped that what the fallen angel had done to her in the cave had been temporary, but it was clear she had been turned into something so wicked that she should not—could not—be allowed to live.

For a moment she saw her mother's hands, held out as the tiny child took her first wobbling step. Saw her mother's smile when Ruxandra cried, "Mama." Heard the words of a lullaby, felt the cool breast against her cheek then the warm rush of milk.

I've never remembered that before. I couldn't have been two years old. It doesn't matter. I am not that girl.

Ruxandra straightened. She wasn't cold, despite being barefoot and in a torn dress. A strong wind blew, and it whipped the dress around her, swirling up her bare legs. She watched the horizon grow brighter. It was almost dawn.

She started walking.

The sun was almost at the horizon.

She hoped to find a clearing where she could be hit by as much of the sun as possible. Instead, the best she could do was a small gap between the trees. She looked around, spotted a large tree; its lower trunk was bare of branches. It would do fine. She took off her dress and hung it on another tree beside her. Even naked, she had no discomfort.

I won't be able to hide from the sun now. It will be faster this way. Ruxandra wrapped her hands around the trunk of the tree, squeezing as hard as she could. Fresh tears sprang to her eyes. *It's going to hurt so much.*

Pretend you're back at the convent. Pretend you're doing penance for your sins. Pretend it's merely a beating from Sister Sofia.

All I must do is endure.

The air grew warmer, and the sky glowed bright enough that it made her squint. She closed her eyes tight.

I will pray for Christ's love first. Then I will pray for repentance and hope he is waiting for me.

She hoped he could forgive her. She didn't want to go to hell. Would the demon—the fallen angel—be there? Ruxandra became embarrassed at the thought, as if the creature would think her ungrateful.

She asked, "Do you want to live?" And I said, "Yes."

The warmth grew uncomfortable. She gripped the tree trunk tighter and prayed, "Christ, my God, set my heart on fire with love of you. That in its flame, I may love you with all my heart, all my mind, all my soul, and all my strength, and my neighbor as myself. So that by keeping your commandments, I may glorify you, the giver of every good and perfect gift. Amen."

Set my heart on fire. It was almost funny, given what was about to happen.

Ruxandra remembered the agony from the last time. She swallowed hard and began the Prayer of Repentance, like the old soldier in the cave. She hoped she could face her death as well as he had.

"God, my good and loving Lord, I acknowledge all the sins which I have committed every day in my life, whether in thought, word, or deed. I ask for forgiveness from the depths of my heart for offending you and others and repent of my old ways. Help me by your grace to change, to sin no more, and to walk in the way of righteousness and to praise and glorify your name, Father, Son, and Holy Spirit. Amen."

The sun broke the horizon, and her body was engulfed with pain.

She twisted and contorted as her flesh burned. Her teeth and talons came out as if she would fight the sun. Ruxandra drove her talons into the tree, refusing to let go. She would die and be done with it. She opened her mouth to pray, but the pain was so awful it took her breath away. She forced more air into her lungs and screamed, "O Lord, my God, I confess that I have sinned against you in thought, word, and deed! I have also omitted to do what your holy law requires of me! But now, with repentance and contrition, I turn again to your love and mercy! I entreat you to forgive me all my transgressions—"

Darkness.

She was surrounded by darkness, cocooned in it.

Is this limbo?

She could hear nothing, see nothing. She had expected to open her eyes to see the fires of hell or the gates of heaven or even the gray plains of Limbo where the dead wandered, forever denied the presence of God. But there was only darkness.

She sighed and turned her head. It moved only an inch before coming up against hard earth.

What?

She dug with one hand, found cold dirt beneath her fingers.

I'm buried alive?

Panic, raw and wild, tore through her body, driving her into frantic motion. She began scrabbling with her hands, talons ripping through the earth. She screamed and thrashed. Dirt filled her mouth. She spat it out and screamed again. Her clawed hands ripped and tore at the earth around her until one broke through into open air. She pushed hard, shoveled hard, trying to clear her body from its tomb of earth.

Then her head was free, and she sucked in cold winter air.

Above her, the moon shone down with a cold, unforgiving light. Her dress still hung on the branch where she had left it. In front of her was the tree she had gripped. Its bark was shredded where she had ripped her talons free. There was a patch of snow, pressed down where she had knelt, and dirt flung in all directions around her grave.

I buried myself?
I thought I had died.
I wanted to die.

CHAPTER
SEVEN

How could I have buried myself?

Ruxandra pulled and crawled her way out of the hole. The movement ignited a dozen fires in her back and legs where the sun had scorched her. Behind her, the earth fell in clumps into the empty grave that should have been hers.

I must have dug the hole while I was burning. I must have pulled the earth over me and hid in the ground until the sun was gone.

The idea that her body could act on its own, even after she had fallen unconscious, was terrifying.

She limped away, brushing the dirt from her flesh. It hurt to touch her legs. She twisted to look; burned, blistered skin ran from her calves as far up her legs as she could see. She continued brushing at the dirt, despite how much it hurt. The pain was her penance and no less than she deserved for what she had done— what she had become.

The torn dress was still hanging from the branch. She glared at it. It was a human thing, and she wasn't human anymore. She was a *thing*. And *things* didn't wear clothes. She should just leave it and walk away.

Except she didn't *want* to be a thing.

She didn't want to lose her humanity even if she was some sort of demon. She took the dress and pulled it over her head. She tried to pull the cloth over her exposed breast but had nothing to secure it with. If she had a needle, she could have sewn it. It wouldn't have been pretty because she was not the best at sewing, but it would be serviceable.

Valeria had always teased her for that. The tall, thin girl would look over her shoulder and point at the stitches until Ruxandra would tickle her to make her go away.

I wonder what she would say now.

if I hadn't been made into a monster, I wouldn't need to sew it in the first place.

Ruxandra shook her head. Self-pity would not help. The main thing was to get as far away from people as she could manage. She glanced at the ground, finding her footprints and the broken branches and torn underbrush that marked the way she had come. She turned her back on them and began walking in the other direction.

The bare branches of the trees and the frozen grass peeking up from the snow stood out stark and hard in the icy winter night. The nipple on her almost bare breast grew hard, but the skin did not burn, nor did she begin to feel numb. Having become a demon, she could no longer be hurt by the cold.

Which is strange, because demons come from the fires of hell. You would think they'd be more used to that than the cold.

Unless that's part of their torment.

Part of my torment.

Unable to stand the sun—a creature of the cold and the dark—she would live in the night, while other people slept. It was an effective way of isolating someone from the world.

How we loved to stay up late whispering when we were eight and nine! Adela, Valeria, and I—back when all the little girls slept together—crowded by the window to see the full moon. Thinking we were so very, very bad.

What are they doing now, my friends?

She had never felt so alone. She had never known one *could* feel so alone.

And this is my forever, night upon night upon night . . .

I cannot bear it . . .

But I can't be near people, not anymore. So accept it and pray, and maybe God will help me escape this miserable existence.

She said the Prayer of Repentance again, repeating it as she walked. The cadence of it became the cadence of her steps. The rise and fall of it became the rhythm of her breath. And with each repetition, she walked farther into the forest until she had no idea where she was. She wasn't even sure if she was still Wallachia.

She was away from other people, and that was all that mattered.

When the sky turned from black to dark blue, Ruxandra looked for shelter. She stepped into gullies and searched around the bottom of trees, hoping to find another overhang or a space in the roots of the tree or a hollowed-out bit of earth where she could hide. She had no doubt she could dig another hole if her body willed it, but she desperately did not want to do that.

Finally she found a spot, a hollowed-out bit of earth beneath the roots of an old oak tree. The space wasn't deep enough to hide her entire body, but time was running out.

She dug at the frozen earth but couldn't gain purchase on the hardened soil. She glanced at the lightening sky, wishing for a shovel, or a knife, or even a sharp stick to make the earth crumble enough to move it.

I had talons in the cave. Why don't I have them now?

With that thought, her fingernails shifted and grew and changed color to long, silver talons that glinted in the pale light of the moon. They didn't look like flesh or fingernails. More like steel daggers, piercing from her skin.

Ruxandra screamed.

In her mind she saw her talons digging into her father's neck. She saw his face contorting, heard his scream before his head tore from his shoulders.

No!

Ruxandra slammed her talons into the frozen earth. They went through as if the dirt were warm lard, digging in with no effort at all. She tore at it, scattering it away from her. Again and again she attacked the ground, putting all her anger and self-hatred into the motions until she had dug a deep, hollow space to hide from the sun. When it was done, and she no longer had need of them, her talons blurred and shrank and became simple fingernails again. She ran the digits one over the other, looking for some hint of the blades beneath but found nothing. It was as if she were an ordinary girl.

Only I'll never be ordinary again.

Ruxandra curled into a ball in the deepest part of her little hollow and stayed there until sleep took her.

She awoke before full dark. The sun was gone from the sky, but there was still light. The red and gold was almost too bright for her to look at, streaming through the few clouds above the trees. On the other side, the sky turned deep blue, then black. Ruxandra stood at the base of her tree, watching. The night was still bright to her eyes, and the stars seemed to shine much brighter than they had before. Even with the moon shining its light upon the earth, she made out the deep blues and grays and dark greens that were the true colors of the night sky.

Beautiful.

I wish . . .

She left the thought unfinished. Instead, she watched the trees as the moon's silver reflection bounced off the snow and glinted along the sleeves of ice encasing their bark. The trees shimmered with their own light, she realized. A deep, drowsy light, as if they waited until spring to wake and shine. She turned in a slow circle, taking in the glow. On one branch, something glowed brighter—a white owl, watching her with wide eyes. Something else slipped across the forest floor—a squirrel, dashing from one tree to the next. Ruxandra knelt beneath her tree, wide-eyed.

She could hear a squirrel—silent to any normal person— skittering up a tree trunk. The owl huffed in a breath, its heart beating faster than a human's. Ruxandra closed her eyes and listened. There were a dozen other small hearts beating nearby, other wings, floating and flapping through the forest, and little feet skittering nearby. Farther off, the hooves of deer tapped against hard earth and the near-silent paws of wolves, padded after them in the dusk.

Ruxandra opened her eyes, then shifted them to the sky again.

It is all so beautiful; so divine.

Why did I have to become a monster to see all this?

She had no answer, so she clasped her hands in front of her and prayed for forgiveness. She prayed for guidance and understanding of what she had become. She prayed to not hurt anyone else, ever again.

She was still praying when the sky lightened, and she was driven once more into the earth to sleep and hide until darkness came again.

When she came out the next night, she was hungry.

It was only the stirring of hunger. The first, lightest pang. And with it came absolute terror.

I will not.

Please, God, do not let me kill again.

Her prayers became frantic; desperate cries to God to give her the strength to resist the hunger until she withered away into nothingness. She forced herself to stay on her knees. She clenched her hands tight and prayed out loud, hoping the noise would drown out her hunger. She tried to focus only on God and his divine works so that she might not kill again and find redemption.

When the sun neared the horizon, she retreated once more into her cave. She wrapped both hands around her belly and curled into a ball. She let sleep take her and hoped it would be enough.

It wasn't.

She awoke ravenous. Her body screamed its hunger at her, desperate for her to fill it. She closed her eyes and tried to pray, but every time she did, Lusa's neck was ready and waiting for her. She could smell the sweat on the woman's body, could feel the woman's heart beating, and when she sank her teeth in, she could taste—

"No!" Ruxandra dropped to the earth, pushing her face hard against the dirt, rubbing it back and forth as if the pain and the cold might somehow drive the hunger away. *Please, God, don't let me do this. Please, God, don't let me do this. Please, God, don't let me do this.*

She could trace her steps back to the village. She was sure of it. She could be there well before sunrise if she ran, and when she got there—

"No! I won't! You hear me? I won't do it! I will not kill another!"

The scream was so loud it startled the birds in the trees and sent a squirrel skittering out and leaping from one frozen branch to the next.

Squirrel.

Ruxandra pulled her face from the earth and listened. There was a squirrel in a tree, not twenty yards from her and still fat from its autumn gorge of nuts. It stared back at her with black, curious eyes. Its claws were dug into the tree, its entire body tense and ready to run away the moment Ruxandra moved.

God gave man dominion over every living thing that walks on the earth. She could hear the squirrel's little heart racing. *I can feed off the squirrel.*

If I can catch it.

She straightened slowly. She wasn't a hunter. She didn't know how to hunt like the men who used to bring deer to her father's court. She had no idea how to move so she wouldn't startle the squirrel. So she ran.

As fast as her legs could take her she ran, racing to the tree and jumping for the branch where the squirrel sat. The squirrel saw her coming and was gone long before she reached the tree. It scrabbled higher up to sit among branches too thin to support the girl's weight.

Ruxandra growled. She turned her back to the tree, then sat down hard. She had to eat, had to catch something before her body drove her back to the village. She glared at the squirrel a moment longer then closed her eyes and listened.

There was another fast and light heartbeat less than a dozen yards away. Ruxandra opened her eyes and stared until she spotted the rabbit under a patch of brambles. It watched her too. She climbed to her feet again. Instead of going toward the rabbit, she angled sideways. The rabbit stayed in its hiding spot. Ruxandra drew closer until she was no more than five yards away.

She turned and sprang, overshooting the rabbit by thirty feet.

Ruxandra was so surprised by how far she'd jumped that she lost her balance and fell, face-first, onto the ground.

The rabbit sprinted away, heading for the woods.

Ruxandra scrambled to her feet and chased after the rabbit, a flash of brown fur and long ears amid the white of the ground. Its feet kicked up little puffs of snow as it dashed away from her. Ruxandra sped up, crashing into trees and jumping over under-brush. She lost her balance twice more and jumped past the rabbit several times.

The rabbit weaved through the trees, changing directions a dozen times. It dove into one side of a bush and raced out the other. It ducked under a fallen tree, changed direction and shot between Ruxandra's legs. She tried to grab the creature and fell over, spinning and crashing into a tree. She yelped, then jumped to her feet. The rabbit dashed farther into the underbrush. Ruxandra chased it, heedless of the scratches and tears to her dress and slapping branches that threatened to hit her eyes.

The rabbit slowed, changing direction more often to confuse her and stay out of her grasp. Ruxandra got within arm's length, lost sight of it, found it again, and came closer and closer.

Then the rabbit jumped the wrong direction, and Ruxandra's hand caught one of its legs.

The rabbit kicked furiously, struggling to escape her grip. Ruxandra grabbed its neck with her other hand and stretched it long. The rabbit screamed. It was a terrible sound, like a child in agony. It was almost enough to make Ruxandra drop the poor creature.

Instead, she sank her teeth into its throat.

The blood slipped down her throat. It wasn't enough. Nowhere near enough. But it was warm and filled with the rabbit's desperate struggle for life. Ruxandra savored every drop as she sucked on the rabbit's neck. The life faded from the creature, becoming a small, limp handful of fur.

Such a little life.

She gently laid the rabbit on the ground and looked around. She had no idea where she was. The woods were thicker and dense with underbrush. A large river roared and rumbled despite the cold.

She closed her eyes again, trying to ignore the river, listening instead for the heartbeats of small animals. There had to be more somewhere. If she could just—

There.

She moved slowly, listening hard. The one was beneath the snow and smaller even than the rabbit. She walked until she was sure she was right above it, then plunged her hand into the snow, grabbing hard and fast and ending up with a handful of furry rage.

The weasel sank its teeth into her, thrashing its head back and forth to rip her skin. Ruxandra screamed and dropped it. The weasel ran across the snow and disappeared. Ruxandra cradled her hand and gritted her teeth until the wound healed. By then, the weasel was too far to be worth chasing even if she were willing to risk being bitten again.

Ruxandra was still hungry. She closed her eyes, listened again, and then began walking.

The river grew louder, making it harder to listen for heartbeats, but Ruxandra was certain of one close by. She was rewarded with a flash of movement as another rabbit dashed out from under cover and ran from her. She chased again, doing a better job of avoiding the trees and the underbrush. The rabbit zigged and zagged and the river grew louder in her ears. She caught glimpses of it between the trees. It was wide and gray with snow. Its water raced between the walls of the ravine, roaring as it went.

The rabbit ran straight for it.

Ruxandra put on a burst of speed and reached for the animal, determined to drink it. The rabbit changed direction right at the edge of the river.

Ruxandra tried to do the same but had too much momentum. Her feet skidded on the snow. She flung out an arm, trying to find something to grasp, but her fingers closed over air, and she plunged into the river.

CHAPTER

EIGHT

RUXANDRA HIT THE WATER—colder than the night air or snowy ground—like a stone. The current grabbed and held her fast, dragging her through the water. She pulled at the water and tried to break the surface, but the river was stronger than she was. It dragged her mercilessly on, ripping her skin on rock and fallen branches. Part of her hair got caught on something, twisted, and tore from her head, making her scream into the racing water.

Her talons came out and ripped along the rocks as she struggled to gain control. The water around her became frothier and obscured her vision. She slammed into a rock, then another, tearing skin and spilling blood into the raging water.

Then her head was above water, and she fell through the air.

The waterfall was high enough that Ruxandra saw the rocks below before the water drove her into them. Her head, back, and legs hit hard. Pain lanced through her. She thought something had snapped. The water grabbed her again, driving her off the rocks and deep into the water and shoving her down with the force of a thousand hands. The pressure flattened her against the bottom of the river and held her there. She struggled and managed to turn upward to see the surface of the water, thirty feet above. The pressure was too much, the water too strong. It would not let her go.

I am going to die.

Thank God.

Instead of terrifying her as it once might have, the thought calmed her. With a deliberate slowness, she blew out all the air in her lungs, watching the bubbles rise and get caught in the whirling maelstrom above her. When there was nothing left, Ruxandra closed her eyes and waited for her body to breathe in the river water. It would hurt, and she would struggle, but it would not last long. Then she would be free.

She waited.

And waited.

And waited.

She opened her eyes. She was still underwater, still trapped beneath the waterfall. She lay, unable to move, not breathing, and still alive. Her body wasn't desperate for air. There was no sudden gulp of water or overwhelming urge to inhale. She was lying there, cold and submerged, but alive.

No. I want to die.

Inside her stomach, as if in answer, the hunger stirred again.

I must get out from here. I must find more rabbits. Or squirrels. Or something. So I don't—

The pain in her body vanished as the broken parts healed themselves. She dug her talons into the riverbed beneath her and used them to pull herself along. It was a slow, painstaking process, moving only inches at a time as the river pounded down on her.

Several large branches smashed through the water's surface above her. One almost touched her before its own buoyancy took it away. She kept creeping forward, and the pressure of the falls grew less and less. Then she was free. The current grabbed at her, twisting her back and forth. She dug her hands deeper into the river bottom to keep her grip.

When her head broke the water for the first time, the frozen, ice-covered trees and cold, rocky ground were the most welcome sights she had ever seen.

She struggled to her feet, exhausted, and stumbled away from the river's edge looking for a place to hide. As the sky began to lighten, she dug a hole in the side of a gully, between the roots of a tree. When the hole was deep enough that no light could reach her, she slept.

When she woke up, she couldn't move.

For a moment she panicked, certain something was wrong with her body—that she had damaged herself beyond repair. She forced her arms to move, to rise from the ground. They jerked free with a tearing of cloth.

Her dress was frozen stiff. It had stuck to her skin and the ground.

She began laughing. A soft, helpless, almost hysterical laugh that filled the hole and stayed just on the edge of sobbing. *Of all the stupid things to happen.*

Ruxandra rocked back and forth, listening to the ice in the dress crackle and tear as it broke free of the ground. She kept at it until she was free and the dress was almost soft. Then she rose and slipped away.

The hunting went slowly. Rabbits were fast and hard to track. She caught one but lost three. Squirrels were worse because they could climb trees faster than she could run.

By the time the sky started to change color for morning, she'd drunk six rabbits and four squirrels. Rabbits tasted better. She liked the fast pulse of their lives; the thin, skittering delight she could feel as a memory in the terrified flesh. Squirrels were more ordinary. There was caution and craftiness in their blood. But either one was fine. Her belly was full and satiated. She made her way back to the cave.

Perhaps I can survive this way.

If I could survive this way, I won't be a monster anymore. I can be a hermit, living in the woods and praying until I die.

It's going to take a lot of rabbits though.

If I can last until spring, it will be easier. There's always lots of game in the spring.

The very idea of spring seemed impossible. The thought that the snow would vanish and the world would ever be warm again seemed ridiculous to her as she headed back to the dark, cold lair she had fashioned. It would happen; she knew as much. At that moment, with the ice from her dress pricking her skin and the cold, hard ground beneath her feet, it seemed so far away.

Something growled.

Ruxandra froze. Her eyes darted back and forth. Shapes hid in the underbrush, long shapes with fur camouflaging them in the dark woods.

I wasn't paying attention. I should have noticed them before.

She turned in a slow circle, watching as they moved into sight. Wolves.

They were lean, all bones and muscle. Their mottled hair went from white to gray to dark brown to near black. Their brown eyes shone with intelligence. Their white teeth gleamed in the darkness. There were twelve of them, surrounding her on three sides, blocking her from her cave.

As one, they growled.

Ruxandra swallowed hard. The wolves on the sides stayed where they were, watching her. In front of her, three stepped out of the shadows and into full view. They were larger than the others. Their muscles rippled under their fur as they walked forward. Their growls grew louder. Then the middle one, a large female with deep brown fur, stepped forward. Her lips pulled back, revealing teeth as sharp and dangerous as Ruxandra's. She snarled, sending shivers of fear through Ruxandra.

Why haven't they attacked?

The lead wolf snarled again and tossed her head. Ruxandra stumbled back a step, then another. The wolf matched her steps, going one forward for each that Ruxandra went back. Along the sides, the other wolves faded back.

They know what I am. The realization shook Ruxandra to the core. *They know I'm not human. That I'm a demon. And they don't want me in their territory.*

Eating all the rabbits.

Ruxandra almost started giggling. She couldn't help herself. Of all the strange and ridiculous things that had happened to her, this was by far the strangest.

The lead wolf snarled again, and the humor of the situation vanished. Ruxandra kept backing away. The wolves on either side spread out and formed a line that reached wide across the forest. The wolves following her drew even with the line and stopped.

It's the edge of their territory. They're showing me that I am not allowed past this point.

She kept walking backward, her eyes on the wolves until she was well away from them. Then she turned and ran.

They outnumber me twelve to one. She dodged trees and jumped over underbrush. *They could have attacked me if they wanted, but they didn't. Am I that powerful?*

The thought was both intoxicating and horrifying.

No! She forced it from her mind and kept running. Dawn was coming, and she needed to find new shelter before the sun broke the horizon. *I will be a holy hermit. I will live off the bounty God provides and spend my nights in prayer until I die.*

It took Ruxandra a month to figure out how to stalk prey, rather than just chase it so they made no sound on the forest floor.

But hunger was a good teacher and was far older and wiser than she.

She had other help, too, though her helpers didn't know it. She watched the foxes and the weasels slip through the night, creep up on their prey, then leap forward with lightning-fast attacks. She watched how their feet moved on the snow, how they inched forward until they were within striking distance.

And when she was not hunting, she was praying.

Though she could not stand the sun, she saw her dark world with crystal clarity. She witnessed the beauty of the stars in their dance above her head, and the slow progress of the moon, from sliver to shining ball to darkness and back to sliver. She saw the crystals of the snow and the reflection of the moonlight in ice, and the still, perfect shapes of the sleeping trees. And she gave thanks to God for each moment.

And in watching the world, Ruxandra learned she could sit still for hours, none of her muscles hurting or twitching or going to sleep. She could stand like a tree, observing the play of hunter and hunted until she knew the pace and pattern of each animal. She saw that the rabbit's moves contrasted the fox's and that the weasel and the field mouse each had a skill the other lacked.

Ruxandra remembered the old nun, Sister Agathe, saying that God made every creature one by one, down to the whiskers, and she had been right. They all glimmered with the perfection of their making, their exquisite adaption to the snow, the woods, the myriad hiding places, each other. She prayed her thanks to God for letting her see this, too.

Then the game grew scarce. The rabbits and squirrels were all gone. The weasels and foxes had left too. There was no food to be had.

One night, she dreamed.

She was in her bed, in her room in the convent. She and Adela were entwined together, and Adela's fingers thrust hard into her, making her moan. Adela put a hand over her mouth to keep her quiet, but it didn't work. The door slammed open, and Sister Sofia was there, leather strap in hand. She pointed at Adela, who slipped out of Ruxandra and out of bed, then knelt on the floor, her bare back ready for Sister Sofia's strap.

"Stop," Ruxandra said.

"No." Sister Sofia raised the strap. "Harlots must be punished."

"*Do not hurt my friends!*"

Ruxandra crossed the room before Sofia could blink. She grabbed the older woman and pulled her close, sinking her fangs deep into her throat. In the background, she heard screaming. She turned, dragging Sister Sofia around so she wouldn't have to stop drinking. Adela scrabbled back to the corner of the room, screaming again and again. Ruxandra dropped Sister Sofia and advanced on her friend.

"Shhh," Ruxandra whispered. "Do not worry. I can make you so strong that she'll never hurt you again."

Adela's scream was loud and long and startled Ruxandra awake.

Outside, a cold, hard wind blew, sending snow swirling and twisting through the air. Above her head were the roots of the tree that sheltered her. In her stomach, the hunger grew.

Images sprang in her head: Lusa. Adela's naked body. Valeria moaning and grabbing at her flesh. Each one's neck was so round and warm, the flow of blood running beneath so strong and full of magic.

The sun was still in the sky. She had to sit there, haunted by memory and images of what could be and the rumbling of a hunger that would become unstoppable. When the sun set, Ruxandra stepped out of the den and began walking.

She kept her ears and eyes and nose open. She knew the smells of the forest now. She could tell at a hundred yards where there might be rabbits or squirrels. She could avoid the packs of wolves that ran in the mountains. She knew the smell of bear and could tell when a cave or overhang was actually a den. She steered clear of the bears the way she steered clear of the wolves. She had no desire to fight anything, especially not something four times her size with bigger claws and teeth.

She prayed as she walked through the night, asking God to guide her. Her den, small and familiar and safe, was soon far behind her. She scented a rabbit and stalked it. She pounced on it and drank it. The hot red blood and the little beast's struggles as its life faded sent a wave of pleasure through her. She wanted more—needed more—but the night was almost gone.

This time, she dug her lair in the side of a hill. She lived there for another month, hunting squirrels and rabbits. She had become good enough at it that she had time to spare. Some nights, she was actually bored. She attended harder to her prayers, but they were not enough to still her mind.

On those occasions she took to practicing her Latin, or doing sums, or recalling stories. For some reason, they were hard to remember. The prayers she did every day stayed in her head. Anything else that she had done before she became what she was grew hazy, as if it were a dream.

When the game had moved on, so did she. That became the pattern of her life. A few weeks in one place, then food would go short, and she would move again.

Around her, the world thawed.

She noticed it first in the air. The cold lessened. The nights grew shorter, though they were by no means short. The crisp hardness of snow vanished, replaced by soft, squishing mud. And by the time she moved to her next spot, the ground she had to dig through to make her cave was nearly thawed. Buds appeared on the trees—small, fragile bits of green amid the brown and gray of early spring.

It rained instead of snowed, leaving Ruxandra wet and miserable. She tried not to go hunting in it, but the hunger drove her into the cold and wet. Those nights, the smarter creatures had found shelter, and she had to dig into their burrows to catch them. She would come home muddy and annoyed, but at least her belly was full.

She prayed a little harder on those nights, hoping God would give her the strength not to feel miserable about it all. It didn't work.

The last of the snow vanished, even from the deepest gullies and darkest ravines. The ground turned green, and the first flowers of the spring bloomed in a profusion of color—red, yellow, orange, and even purple. Ruxandra admired each one, inhaled each one, and tried to avoid crushing them as she hunted. Sometimes the rabbits would go right through them though, and she would chase after. It made her sad when she turned back, but there was nothing to be done. She couldn't let her prey get away for the sake of a few blossoms.

Then she found the pond.

The sun had just gone down. She was following a trail of rabbit tracks. She wasn't a good tracker yet, but she was getting the idea. She followed the tracks up to the water before she realized what she stared at.

The pond was wide and deep, though far too small to be called a lake. A stream flowed in one side and out the other, keeping the water fresh and clean. The edges were surrounded with cattails and tall grass, and Ruxandra found the trails of animals leading up to it. There were rabbit and deer tracks, and mystery tracks she soon determined had been left by a badger. All of them had come there to drink. Ruxandra circled it twice, looking and listening. The rabbit was long gone. Night insects flew over the top of the water, and above them bats swooped down, snapping their teeth. Ruxandra walked down to the edge of the pond and looked in. The water was so clear that Ruxandra could see her reflection.

"Oh dear God," Ruxandra whispered. "What have I become?"

CHAPTER

NINE

T HE WOMAN REFLECTED in the water was filthy—so filthy that Ruxandra could barely see her skin. Blood and dirt coated her face in a thick layer and ran in dark brown streaks down her neck and shoulders. Ruxandra raised one hand and rubbed at her cheek, but it wouldn't come clean. The grime was thick and embedded in her flesh. Her hair hung in tangled mats. It looked less like hair than wet, unteased wool, shorn from a sheep and then left in a pile for a week.

"This isn't me."

The strength left her legs, and she fell into the mud beside the pond.

I haven't become something holy. I haven't become a servant of God. I've become something filthy and vile. A shiver ran through her, from head to foot. She couldn't remember the last time she'd been in water.

I cannot be like this. I am not a beast. I'm not. I must get clean.

She shoved her hands into the water. It was cold, almost as cold as the river had been. She scrubbed, rubbing hard against the skin. The first layer of dirt and blood came off, but the next layer stayed, clinging to her skin like it had been tattooed.

In desperation, she picked up a handful of mud and began rubbing it against her skin, letting the coarseness of the dirt abrade and scrape her arms clean. Five times she rubbed the mud. Five times she splashed water on it. Still, it wasn't clean.

It won't come off.

Ruxandra threw herself into the pond.

The water wrapped around her, cold enough to freeze every muscle in her body but only for a moment. She pulled her head above the surface, her matted hair flinging and sending water flying. She got her legs under her and struggled gain traction on the slimy mud beneath. Her feet slipped and sank. For a moment she thought she might sink in, might lay entombed and trapped forever. Then she found firm footing. She attacked her arms again, squatting below the surface to grab more mud to rub the filth from her flesh. Again and again, she dunked until both arms were clean.

A breeze rippled the water of the pond. It flowed over the wet cloth of her dress, pulling away what warmth was left in her. She looked down and for the first time realized how filthy the dress had become.

Blood, dirt, and other stains Ruxandra couldn't guess at covered the fabric. Even soaked through, it felt crusty. She grabbed at the wet cloth and tried to pull it off. It clung like a snake wrapped around its prey, not wanting to let go. She pulled hard at it and heard a seam rip. It was almost enough to make her cry. She had to get it off, had to get the vile thing away from her flesh. But it was the only clothing she had. She couldn't afford to destroy it.

"Calm down!" *I'm not a beast. I need the clothes.* She forced her hands down before she ripped the dress more. "It will come off. Go slow and it will come off."

She wriggled one arm inside the dress, then the other. She shimmied and twisted and gathered the fabric together until she found the bottom seam. Then she lifted, pushing and pulling the dress up and over her head. The wet fabric protested every inch. It didn't want to separate from her skin. And when it was around her head, the dress tangled on her matted hair. She shook her head back and forth, desperate to escape the wet, clinging fabric. Then her hair gave way, and the dress slipped off. She threw it onto the shore and began scrubbing at her flesh again.

Her legs were the easiest. There was little blood on them, only worn-in dirt that she scrubbed until both her legs were bright red. Her body came next. She had lost weight, she realized. She had been slightly plump before. And while her breasts were still firm and large, and the muscles all still there, everywhere else the fat had gone, leaving her body carved and lean as stone.

Her dress had caught most of the dirt and blood, and her body came clean with much less effort than it had taken her arms. She scrubbed hard at her face next, dunking it into the water again and again until no more mud or blood were left on the skin.

Ruxandra sank below the water and started on her hair.

It floated in clumps around her head. What she could see looked like the stubby tentacles of some sea creature. She shoved her fingers into it, rubbing back and forth against her scalp. She tried to pull her fingers through her hair, to loosen up the mats, but they didn't release at all. In frustration, she willed her talons out. They pierced into the mess, and Ruxandra could feel them slicing through the strands. She growled in frustration, sending bubbles up above the water, and began hacking into the bird's nest. Lumps of hair floated around her until she looked like she was sitting in a sea of floating hairballs left by a dozen angry, sick cats. By the time she finished cutting the last of them, her hair was a ragged mess.

I must look awful. She broke the surface and ran her fingers through her hair until the last tangle vanished, then rubbed and scrubbed at her scalp until it too felt raw. She dunked under again, then came up. *I'm a complete mess. I know it.*

"Perhaps I am." Ruxandra was amazed how little that worried her. "But I'm clean now, and it's a start."

Hunger tweaked Ruxandra's stomach, reminding her she hadn't eaten yet that evening. She rose out of the water and waded to the shore. The dress lay in a wet heap on the ground. She picked it up with the tips of two fingers. It was still filthy, and the thought of it touching her skin was beyond repulsive.

The cold breeze hit her, sending a shiver up her spine.

"And now I have nothing to wear at all." She sighed. "Or anything to dry myself with. Wonderful. And now what? Must I hunt naked?"

Unless she wanted to put on the stinking, sopping dress, that was her only option. And while it wasn't a thought that appealed to her at all, there really wasn't another choice. And so she carried the dress back to her den and hung it on a tree. With luck, it would be dry enough to wear when she returned. Without luck, she would sleep naked as well.

"And won't that be a delight," she muttered.

She sniffed the air and listened for the sound of small feet and smaller heartbeats, lurking in the underbrush. There were plenty of them around, especially near the pond. She sorted which were rabbits, which were squirrels, and which were weasels or foxes. She went for the rabbits first.

It was odd, moving naked through the forest. The breeze on her skin was at once distracting and invigorating. It teased her breasts and backside, making her nipples hard and her bottom bumpy with gooseflesh. It dried the water from her body, sending shivers over her. Her breasts moved in ways she wasn't used to and bounced so much when she ran that she missed the first rabbit from sheer surprise.

She caught the second one though, sinking her teeth into its neck and feeling the blood spurt against her skin. She sucked in as much of it as she could, but still some escaped, making a mess down her front. She wiped it away with her hands, realized she had nothing to wipe her hands with, and rubbed them on a tree.

Three rabbits later she wanted to wash again.

"I must get better at this," she told the dead rabbit in her hand. "I must waste less blood and make less mess. Meanwhile, I'll wash every night before I return to my den. That will be better."

She caught enough rabbits to fill her stomach and headed home. The sky was growing brighter and brighter as she slipped into her cave—her fourth since the river, she realized. The dress was still wet, of course. So she curled up on the ground, feeling the roughness of the dirt against her skin.

"I should get some hay," she told the roots above her head. "That way I will not have to lie on the dirt like a wild beast."

Just on straw like a tame one. The thought made her chuckle. She curled up into the corner but couldn't get comfortable. Before, she'd barely noticed the ground unless there was a rock under her. Now she was far too aware of how dirty she was getting by lying there. She began to itch in a dozen places. She scratched and scratched, but it did no good. Every time she stopped one itch, three more popped up in its place. "Now I'll have to go back into the pond again tomorrow. Wonderful."

She sighed and rolled over. Then she rolled over again. She spent half the day rolling and scratching and wishing night would hurry up and arrive. By the time she fell into a fitful, itchy sleep, she was convinced that half the insects in the forest had nested on her skin, and the other half were living in her hair.

At least nothing is biting me.

She woke as soon as the sun slipped beneath the horizon. The last light of the day was still bright enough to hurt her eyes. She grabbed her dress and bolted for the pond. She could smell the water, could imagine how it would feel on her skin. It would be soft and would take away the dirt and be so . . .

"Cold. It's going to be cold. But it's not like I feel the cold, so it doesn't matter. And the dress gets washed first. I can manage to get the worst of the stink and dirt out of it. Then I can wear it again tomorrow night."

The pond didn't look any warmer after she said it. It wasn't a hot bath, wasn't even close. But she itched so much that even another cold scrub would be better than a night of being filthy.

"Or perhaps you'd rather stink?" Ruxandra said out loud. "Perhaps you'd rather be a beast?"

Like I was doing before I discovered the pond?

The thought terrified her. She jumped into the middle of the pond, and the cold shock of it drove the idea away. The water, she discovered, was only about eight feet deep.

She walked across the bottom of the pond until she broke the surface. She looked down at her skin. Most of the blood was gone. She scrubbed off the last of it and waded to the shore. Her dress was lying in the mud at the pond's edge.

"And now, it's your turn." She picked up the ragged piece of fabric. "I'll get you clean if it's the last thing I do. Into the water you go!"

She turned and saw a man standing at the edge of the pond.

He was taller than her and wide at the shoulders. He had sandy-brown hair and brown eyes set in a square, strong face that had been tanned by the sun. His clothes were homespun and simple—a jerkin and hose under a long cloak. He had an axe in his hand and a bow and quiver on his back.

And he was staring at her.

I'm naked. The realization worked its way through her mind. *I'm naked, and a man is staring at me.*

A young man, in fact—not much older than she.

A strong, handsome young man is staring at me. And I'm naked.

Ruxandra screamed and dove back into the water.

I'*LL STAY UNDER UNTIL HE GOES away. That's what I'll do.*
Then it occurred to her that he might *not* go away. He might
think she was drowning. And if he thought that, what if he
dove in to help her? He might try to pull her out.

I can't let a man touch me while I'm naked!

Ruxandra pulled herself back to the side of the pond, where
the water was shallow enough to kneel in so only her head was
above the water. She tucked her knees under her and crossed her
arms in front of her breasts.

He was still there, still staring.

"Go away!" The words flew out of Ruxandra in a sharp shriek
that pierced the woods. "Get out of here!"

The young man blushed. The red spread all the way from his
chest to the roots of his hair. He turned his back.

"I'm sorry!" he called over his shoulder. "I didn't know you
were there. I heard the splash and thought it was a bear, and
perhaps I could get some meat or the pelt, so I—"

"Well, it isn't a bear, it's me! Now go away!"

"I will! I will!" He rose to his feet and stumbled a few steps away. "It's just, well . . . Are you hurt?"

"I'm fine! I'm having a bath!"

"I mean . . ." The young man started to turn back, then stopped. "I mean . . . I saw your dress, and it was . . . it had been ripped, and I wondered . . ."

She watched his back tense as he floundered for words, cringing with embarrassment.

But he still saw me naked. She made her voice sharp. "You wondered what? If you could take advantage?"

"No!" His ears were bright red now. "I thought . . . I thought you might be cold and needed help."

"Well, I'm not, and I don't. So go away!"

"I will. But..." He took a pair of steps forward, then stopped. With a quick move he undid his belt and took off his cloak. "Here. Take it. You'll be warmer in it."

"I told you—"

"I can bring you some other things." His voice sped up with every word as if he needed to rush them all out before his throat closed. "I *will* bring you some other things. You keep the cloak for now, and I'll return in a few days."

He hung the cloak on a low branch. "There. I promise I won't peek. I'll go away."

Ruxandra listened to his footsteps as he weaved through the brush. She waited a long time until there were only whispers of movement in the underbrush. She crept around the edge of the pond, her eyes wide and searching.

There was no sign of him.

She raised the cloak off its branch. It was wool—but not expensive wool like she had worn in the convent. It was homespun.

This wool was rough and itchy. But it was clean and warm, and it would be something to keep between her and the ground at night.

Ruxandra hesitated a moment longer. Then she wrapped it around her body.

To her surprise, the inside of the cloak had been lined with soft linen. It caressed her skin, keeping the wool from scratching her. She wrapped it tight around her body and for the first time in— *Weeks? Months?*—felt warm. It was not that the cold ever hurt her. Most nights she didn't mind it at all. But to be wrapped in warm, soft cloth was comforting, like the kitchen fire on a cold night in the convent.

She slipped her arms through the slits on the sides, hugging herself. She spun, letting it flare, then saw her old dress on the ground.

"I must finish cleaning you," she said. "This cloak is so nice but I'll have to give this back when he returns. So I'd better keep washing you."

Reluctantly she walked around the pond. She almost picked up the dress, but realized she would get the cloak wet if she did. With reluctance, she took the cloak off and hung it on another branch. Then she knelt beside the pond, grabbed her dress, and then started scrubbing. It took hours to get the worst of the filth out. Even then the dress was so stained that Ruxandra could hardly tell its original color. She wrapped herself in the cloak and carried the dress back to her den. The sky wasn't turning blue yet, but it would soon.

"It's too late for hunting," she told the dress as she hung it on the branch. She ran her hands over the cloak. She didn't want to get it too dirty. That would ruin it. "But not too late to make something of a bed, is it?"

Branches were the easiest thing, Ruxandra decided. She went tree to tree and pulled small limbs from them. It was difficult. The trees were green with spring; they wanted to bend rather than break. She ended up using her talons to hack through the tree limbs. She took them all back to her den, broke the big ones to fit them inside, and began to lay them on the floor. She stared at the pile, uncertain how to proceed.

"Green!" she realized. "The wood is green. It bent. I bet I can weave it."

She picked up the longest branches, laid them out in a square, and began crisscrossing the others. It wasn't hard for her to bend and weave the branches back and forth. The same strength that allowed her to tear them from the trees made it easy to weave them like straw. She wished she had someone to show it to. Perhaps the man who had seen her—

I can't show a man my room! She looked at the dirt walls of the den. *And I certainly cannot tell him I've been living in the woods, being a hermit. He wouldn't understand.*

She went back to the work. The sun was up outside her den by the time she had the bed frame finished to her satisfaction. It was only a few inches off the ground, but it was off the ground.

"I can sleep like a person again," she told it. "And I even have a blanket!"

Ruxandra laid the cloak over the frame and sat on it. The bed was a bit bumpy but so much better and cleaner than the floor. She wrapped the cloak around her body and snuggled in.

"He's coming back," she whispered to the den walls. "Soon."

The thought of seeing him again—seeing the way blood rushed to his face when he blushed—made her absurdly happy.

Made her hungry.

"No!" Ruxandra sat up fast and hard. "I won't do that to him! I don't need to!"

She threw herself back down in the bed and pulled the cloak tight about her.

"I don't," she whispered to herself. "I don't, I don't, I don't, I don't."

She began praying again, harder than she'd ever prayed before.

The next night, she left the cloak in the cave. She almost put the dress on, but decided against that too. It wouldn't do to get it bloody again. Hunting naked was better. She would hunt until she was full, and then she would clean up at the pond.

"He said he would be gone a few days. So I can wash up at the pond and not be seen," She frowned. "Perhaps I should bring the dress anyway and keep it close by, in case he returns."

She compromised by hanging the dress by the pond, then going hunting. She ended up eating squirrels that night. They weren't as filling as rabbits, and their blood didn't have the same fizz, but she found enough to make her content. Then she went back to the pool and bathed. This time, she paid attention and kept her ears and eyes and nose wide open, looking for any sign of him. She hurried through her bath, and stood drying for as long as she dared before taking the dress and going back to her den.

She stared at the abused fabric, the rip over one breast and the torn seams from when she had frozen to the ground. There was no way she could repair it. Nothing she could do would make it look better or even decent.

"Perhaps he can bring me some sewing supplies." She crawled into his cloak and nestled in. It smelled like him, which she liked. A very masculine smell that was so different from the way the girls at the convent smelled. It stirred things inside her.

It also stirred the hunger, but Ruxandra clamped down on it. As long as she was full, it wouldn't be a problem.

But what if I run out of rabbits and squirrels before he comes back?

She found the answer the next night, in the hour between sunset and the sky going dark.

She smelled them first—two dozen musky, earthy scents that spoke of forest and grass and trees. She followed the aroma to a glade and found the ground matted and torn, fresh hoofprints in the mud.

Deer.

I can't take on a full-size deer.

But a small one . . .

She found the fawn nestled in the bushes. She looked for its mother, but the doe was nowhere to be seen. The poor little creature trembled in terror but didn't move, relying on its camouflage to keep it safe. It didn't help. Ruxandra grabbed it and sank her teeth deep into the little thing's neck. It tried to kick at her and cried for its mother, but Ruxandra clamped its mouth shut.

There was so much more life in the deer than there had been in the rabbits. She realized she'd never had a creature so young: the rabbits and squirrels bore litters, but she didn't bother with their babies; they were too small. But the fawn was large enough, and drinking it gave her a definite springy feel. Like spring onions and lettuces. She almost laughed as she drank, thinking how she would explain her kill to any other person.

When she was done, she was full—more full than she had ever felt on rabbits. She laid the little body down, then ran back to the pond. Again she watched, but there was no sign of the young man.

"I wonder where he came from," she asked the cattails at the edge of the water. "Well, I know one way to find out." She started in the direction she'd seen him last go, and wondered if she was heading toward a village.

It doesn't matter. I'll be fine.

She was full. She had no desire to hunt anything, she told herself, even if she did come across people. Besides, if she saw anyone, she could run away and hide in the woods. That would be easy enough. She'd become much better at hiding in the past few months.

The farther she went, the more trees were cut, until she came to a clearing of stumps with a small, solid log hut in the middle.

"He's a woodcutter," she said through a breathy exhale. "And this is where he stays when he's collecting the wood. I bet he has a cart that he uses to take the wood back to town."

She stopped talking and listened. The forest was filled with its night sounds: the flutter of bat wings and the slower, more graceful strokes of an owl. Little creatures slipped beneath the leaves and grass, and larger ones moved between the trees. The breeze blew the leaves above her, making them rustle and whisper, but there was no sound inside the little cabin.

"He must have gone back into town," she decided. "Otherwise, he'd be here with his cart."

She circled the cabin and found a wider trail with two deep ruts where wheels had dug into the ground. She thought about following it but didn't. The ruts would lead back to his village. And that would mean people.

But he's people, isn't he?

"He's different. There's only one of him. If I keep my distance, I'll be fine." She glanced back to the hut and bit her lip. "But I'm sure he wouldn't mind if I looked inside."

Though she knew it was empty, she knocked. "It's only polite, after all."

The door moved when her knuckles hit it. She pushed it open, then peered inside.

It was one room. A fire pit sat in the middle, and a thick straw mattress was to the side. There were plain wooden shelves that held wooden plates and cups and some wooden spoons. There were hooks for hanging his clothes and bow and a small table with two chairs. It was a tight, crowded little place, and Ruxandra was enchanted by it.

It smelled like him.

She sensed his presence on the chairs—no, on one chair. The one facing the door. She could smell where his hands had rested on the table and where he had sat before the fire pit. She could smell him on the mattress in the bed.

Oh, the bed.

"I shouldn't," she told herself. "I really shouldn't."

Yet she wanted to so much.

"He isn't here. I'm sure he will not mind."

She sat on the bed. Then she lay down, letting the soft straw mattress envelop her. It was far better than her own bed—far better than anything she'd slept on in months. She wriggled and squirmed, feeling the straw shift and move beneath her. It felt so good. And it smelled so much like him.

She closed her eyes and breathed in his scent. It was warm and enticing and sent shivers down her spine in the way Adela used to do when she would lick Ruxandra's ear. Or when Valeria would sneak up behind her and cup her breasts when no one was looking. Ruxandra squirmed again and let one hand drift down her body, caressing breast and belly and slipping between her legs.

I am acting like a beast, she thought, as she began rubbing. *Like a cat in heat.*

She brought up her other hand to caress and pinch at her breasts while she rubbed frantically against her sex. She moaned. Feeling her tension rise higher and higher until she gasped and convulsed on the bed, inhaling his smell as she shuddered through her release.

Oh God, what have I done?

Ruxandra sat up, too embarrassed to stay. She straightened her dress and the mattress, and slipped back into the cool of the spring night. She should pray, she knew. She should calm her mind and calm herself but she couldn't. She wandered through the woods, in a daze of pleasure. She let her eyes and ears and nose drink in all they could until the sky began to lighten. Then she crawled back to her den and, once more, wrapped herself in his cloak.

She dreamed she was in the chapel at the convent, praying for forgiveness. But the fallen angel was there, watching. She was beautiful, with her sharp fangs, womanly shape, and unearthly eyes. The man stood beside her, his strong chest bare, his eyes devouring Ruxandra. She tried to keep praying, but could only think of them; of what it would be like to be touched by them.

When she woke up, she couldn't bring herself to pray anymore.

She went back to the glade instead, and followed the hoof prints until she found another fawn. She drank until she felt full, and rushed back to the pond. She washed off the blood and put on her dress and his cloak in case he came that night.

She heard him first. He was whistling. She didn't recognize the tune. The nuns frowned on any song that wasn't directed to God. From the quick rhythm of his hums, it was a dance tune, and he was likely whistling it to give her warning.

Ruxandra ran her fingers through her still-ragged hair. It was growing back, faster than it used to, but was in no way in good condition. She patted it down the best she could.

But she couldn't bring herself to step into the clearing.

When he came into sight, she stood on the far side of the pond, hidden in the trees. She stared at his strong jawline and the muscles that moved beneath his clothes. She inhaled him—his sweat, his musk, his clothes. She took a step forward and froze.

I am going, all by myself, to greet a man whom I have never met. It was improper, and worse, it was embarrassing. *What in the name of God am I thinking?*

I'm being silly, she told herself. *He's just a man. I am a woman. It is perfectly natural for us to meet and speak. I should not be so worried about appearances. I'm in the forest, for God's sake.*

"Miss? Are you there?" His voice echoed through the forest. "Miss?"

Ruxandra turned and fled.

CHAPTER
ELEVEN

S HE LAY, WRAPPED IN HIS cloak, crying, for the rest of
the night and the entirety of the day.

"Stupid," Ruxandra grumbled to the tree above her. "It's
stupid. I do not know him. So why am I crying? Because I was
too scared to meet him? It's stupid!"

She pulled herself into a tighter ball and closed her eyes,
trying to sleep. It eluded her.

"I shouldn't be scared of him. He's a nice man. He will not
hurt me. Cannot hurt me . . ."

Unless he finds out what I am.

"He doesn't have to find out. It's not as though I'm staying
around here forever, is it? I'll run out of animals, and then I'll—"

I'll drink him.

"No! I'd leave before I would do that. And I'll feed before I
see him so I will not want to drink him."

She was sure that was true. Even if she did want to drink
him—a little bit—she wouldn't have to, the way she *had to* with
the old woman. It would be no worse than those times the nuns

punished her by sending her to her room without supper. She'd gotten used to that, she could get used to this.

She wanted to speak to him. He seemed nice, and she was so, so very lonely.

"Tomorrow night," Ruxandra said, firm. "I'll talk to him tomorrow night."

It didn't stop her from crying, which was still stupid as far as she was concerned.

As soon as the sun vanished, Ruxandra left her clothes and his cloak behind and went searching for prey. There were no fawns nearby, so she had to make do with rabbits, which took longer and squirmed more, so they were messier. By the time she reached the pond, it was well past dark. She looked and listened, but there was no sign of him. There was, however, something that smelled different.

Lilacs?

Lilacs had been everywhere around the convent, and the sweet smell of the little purple flowers was one of the first true signs of spring. Ruxandra had never seen any growing near the pond.

"What am I smelling?"

She sank close to the earth and skulked around the pond. There was no sign of *him*, but there was a wooden chest, lying open under a tree. It wasn't very big, only two feet on each side, with a plain wooden lid held in place by leather straps. She crept closer, and the smell of lilacs grew stronger. Ruxandra peered over the edge of the chest and gasped.

A small bar of soap, the source of the lilac smell, sat on top of a neatly folded green dress. Ruxandra stared at them in delight.

"He left them for me. For me to use and wear."

She almost started crying again. She looked around, hoping to see him somewhere close, but there was no sign of him. "He's gone because I took too long. But I cannot hunt rabbits any faster."

She reached for the dress, to see how soft it was, and saw the blood that coated her hand. She pulled it back fast, terrified of dripping blood on the pretty green wool. With the other hand, which wasn't quite so bloody, she carefully took the soap off the top of the pile, then went back down to the pool to wash. The soap made the blood and dirt slide off her skin and left her smelling so pretty.

When she was clean, she went back to the chest. She didn't want to put the clothes on wet for fear of making the dye in the dress run and stain her skin.

"I'll take the whole chest back to the den. Then I can see what's in it properly."

The chest wasn't heavy at all, and she carried it back to her den with ease. She spread out the cloak on her bed frame and laid the contents of the chest on top of it. The dress was even more beautiful when it was unfolded. It had long, loose sleeves; a square bodice; a gathered waist; and a wide, flowing skirt. It would look amazing on her. And the bodice would show off her breasts very well.

"Especially since I have no chemise. I'm going to have to keep my back straight the entire time I wear it, or he's going to see everything all the way down." She remembered the moment at the pond, and her stomach twisted with embarrassment. "Not that he hasn't seen it all already, but that doesn't mean I should be purposely immodest. Now, what's—oh."

Under the dress were two chemises.

"He really is sweet," Ruxandra whispered. She laid them on the bed. They were simple linen, like the dress, but soft and pretty. Beneath them was another, longer strip of linen that made Ruxandra smile even wider. "And a towel. He thought of everything."

I wonder where he got it all.

"It's probably his sister's old clothes. Or his mother's. He wouldn't have bought them. Not for a stranger."

She picked up one of the chemises and pulled it over her head. The linen was clean and soft and felt wonderful against her skin. She hugged herself, reveling in the feel of the fabric. Then she put on the dress.

It was a little tight in the chest and a little short in the leg, but it fit well enough over her hips, shoulders, and arms. She did up the laces on the front, tied the bow, and spun in a slow circle.

"I bet I look wonderful," she said to the chest. "I wish I had a mirror. It would be perfect if I could see what I look like."

There is the pond.

"Which is good, but I do not want him to see me."

Oh, yes, you do.

Ruxandra blushed at her own thoughts. "Yes, I do. But I don't want him to see me before I'm ready to see him. I mean . . . what if . . ."

I run away again?

"Yes. Except, I won't. Besides, I need to say 'thank you' to him, right?"

If I have the courage.

Why do I care so much anyway?

The thought came out of nowhere but gave her pause. To get her clothes and soap and a comb? He was a wonderful man.

And he was handsome too. Strong, straight arms and legs, a wide chest, and perhaps even—

Those pictures were too large, she scolded herself. *Valeria said so. Now stop it.*

Ruxandra folded the extra chemise and put it in the little chest. She picked up the comb and began working it through her hair. It had grown back much faster than Ruxandra had expected and was now the same length as it had been when she cut it off. That was wonderful. The tangles, however, were not. She spent a good hour pulling the comb through her hair again and again until it was all tangle-free and smooth. She thought about braiding it but left it alone.

"An unmarried young woman's hair should flow freely so her lover will be enticed by it. That's what Adela always said."

You do not have a lover.

"I know I don't have a lover. It's just something Adela said."

Why is he *so important?*

"*I don't know!*" The words came out half as a yell, half as an animal snarl. Ruxandra stumbled back at the sound of them. She hit the bed frame with her calves, lost balance, and fell on her backside on the cloak. She didn't move. She had frightened herself with the sheer animal power of the words. It hadn't sounded like her at all. It hadn't *felt* like her. It felt like the ravaging beast that had slaughtered her father and the others.

It can't be. I'm eating. I'm satisfied. It will all be fine. Her next words came out as a whisper. "But I think I must be very, very careful."

The comb had fallen to the ground. Ruxandra picked it up and with slow, deliberate strokes began combing her hair. She was the daughter of the *voivode* of Wallachia, raised in a convent, and was living as a hermit, dedicated to God. She was *not* a vicious beast.

I'm not. I'm not. I'm not.

When she was done with her hair, she took off her dress, folded it neatly, and put it in the chest. She kept the chemise on because a lady did not sleep naked, even if she was a hermit. They wore clothes, as was proper, and *she* was a proper young lady.

The next evening, she rose and then dressed. She was very hungry but knew that it would grow worse as the evening went on. Even so, she couldn't risk not seeing him. She ran the comb through her hair and put on the dress over the chemise. She did her best to make sure there was no dirt on it. Then she ran to the pond.

It was odd, running in clothes she cared about. With the other dress, it had long since ceased to matter if it snagged on something. This one, though, was new and pretty, and Ruxandra was not going to risk damaging it. So she moved carefully through the woods, going around brush she once charged through. She moved at human speed, rather than her own pace. It was safer for the dress, and if *he* happened to see her, she wouldn't have to explain anything.

If he sees me. What if he's not there?

"Then I'll go to his cabin and knock on the door and introduce myself." Ruxandra ducked under a tree branch, followed an animal path and then went wide around a thornbush. "Like a proper young lady."

She had to fight the urge to pick up her pace. Instead, she slowed. She would approach at a brisk, purposeful walk. The walk of a young lady who knew where she was going and had someone to meet when she got there.

She smelled him.

It froze her in her tracks. Her knees quivered. A warm fluttering, like a butterfly made of smoke and heat, filled her stomach. He smelled the same—warm and strong and so human. She so wanted to see him. She growled with frustration, then slapped a hand over her mouth. *No animal noise, Ruxandra. You do not want to scare him.*

She forced her legs to move again, slow and steady, through the forest. The evening light was fading, and soon it would be dark, and he would go back to his little cottage, and she would miss her chance to see him. But as she approached the pond, her feet dragged. The butterfly fluttered more frantically, and her mouth went dry.

Then she stood at the edge of the pool, hidden behind the thick trunk of a tree, and she could see him.

He had on the same clothes and the same strong muscles and wide chest and divine smell. He stood where he had left the chest. His eyes scanned the woods. She froze. His gaze swept right past her, then back again. He sighed and squatted down, looking at her footprints. They led straight to the pond and back twice. But after that, they would lead him back to her den.

He must not come to the den. He must not see how I'm living. I must talk to him.

He stood up and sighed. He scanned the woods once more. Then he turned his back and headed for the path to his cabin.

Don't let him go! "Wait!"

He spun, eyes darting everywhere. "Where are you?"

Ruxandra stepped back into the darkness.

"Did you like the dress?" he called. "Does it fit?"

Come on, fool. You spoke once. Speak again.

"It was my sister's. She left it when she married the miller. I thought it might fit you."

All I have to do is speak. Then everything will be fine.

"I live in the village." The way he said it made it seem as if his village was the only one. "It's about five miles from here. I collect wood and bring it in for people."

If I speak, I can get close to him. Then we can talk, and perhaps we can—

"Hello?"

Maybe hold hands? Perhaps—

"Are you still there?"

Ruxandra's frustration grew. *He's just a man. Why can I not talk to him?*

"I must rest. May I come see you tomorrow? At noon? I could bring some bread and cheese and . . ." His voice faded. For the first time, he looked sad. He sighed again, and his next words came out quieter. "You're not there, are you?"

"I am!" The words burst out of Ruxandra. "I am here. Right here. And I'll be back at midnight. Tomorrow at midnight. We can talk then. I promise to come out."

The sad look vanished, and his face broke into a wide, happy grin. He had strong teeth too, which shone bright white. "I will be here."

"No coming before that," Ruxandra warned. "I must get cleaned up first."

"I will not."

Her heart caught in her throat. "Promise?"

"I promise."

"I'll see you then," Ruxandra said. "I promise too."

She walked backward into the woods until she lost sight of him. Then she turned and ran. A giggle escaped her lips and then another. He was going to be there. She was going to talk to him.

I'll need to hunt well before midnight. I must be full, so I do not . . . She shuddered at the thought. She went back to the den, slipped off the dress and the chemise, then went out into the woods. *Tonight I'll search for a fawn or a den of young rabbits, then return to the same place tomorrow night to feed. Then I can get cleaned up and be all ready before I meet him.*

It took most of the night, but she found a fawn. It wasn't as small as the last one, but it was still young enough to have its spots and to hide and lie still when it sensed a predator, rather than to jump up and fight. She marked the location in her mind and made a wide circle through the area. She spotted two more nests and noted them as well.

Three days' eating. Three nights where I can hunt fast and clean up and see him.

It will be good. It will be very good.

She slipped back into her den as dawn came. She put on the chemise and, for the second night in a row, went to bed dressed like a proper young lady. She lay there for a long time. The butterfly danced in her stomach again. The anticipation was so strong it kept her from sleep. She rehearsed what she would say and what she would look like when she said it.

When the sun slipped behind the horizon, Ruxandra slipped out into the night. She found the fawn at top speed. It heard her coming but only for a moment before she was on top of it, her teeth sinking into its neck. It bucked and squealed, and she clamped a hand over its throat, cutting off any sound. She put her whole body weight over it and kept drinking and drinking until it went still and the last of its bright, fresh life was gone. She was calmer and more hopeful. Her senses were sharper, and the woods had extra colors, extra layers of sound and scent.

It would be incredible to share this.

She ran back to the den to grab the soap and towel, then to the pool. Her nose told her he was nowhere nearby. She dove into the water and came up scrubbing. She had spilled almost no blood on herself. It took only moments to wash off and moments more to run the soap over the rest of her body. Then it was out of the pool, grab the towel, and race back to the den. She stood outside to dry herself. Then she slipped into the clean chemise and the dress.

At midnight, she was sitting on a log near the pond, watching his lantern waving back and forth as he walked. She took several deep breaths, trying to slow the butterflies in her stomach. It didn't work. He was even more handsome in the yellow light of the lantern. The glow highlighted his features, making them stronger and sharper.

She took another deep breath, made sure the dress was properly arranged, then called, "Hello."

CHAPTER

TWELVE

IS SMILE LOOKED EVEN better up close. He blushed very prettily too.

He swallowed twice before he managed to find his voice. "Hello."

The butterflies fluttered in her stomach again. She cast around for something to say and settled on the obvious. "Thank you for the clothes."

"They're my sister's," he said. "*Were* my sister's. She married the miller, and he gave her new clothes, so she left them at our house, and I thought they might fit you and . . ."

He looked at the ground and scuffed one boot in the dirt and blushed some more. Ruxandra tried not to smile, lest it embarrass him. *At least I'm not the one babbling.* "They fit very well. Though they're a bit tight around the chest."

Oh goodness, why did I say that? She watched as his eyes went to her chest, then slid to the side. She stood up. "They're also a bit short, see?"

He took in her bare feet under the dress. His eyebrows went up. "You do not have shoes?"

"No." Ruxandra stared at her bare toes in the dirt. She'd forgotten about that entirely. "I do not need them. I mean, I haven't worn them in a long time, so my feet are used to being without."

Now I sound like some wild creature of the forest.

He glanced at her face and swallowed. He bowed his head. "I am very sorry for coming on you like that. I had no idea."

"I should think so!" Ruxandra bit her lip at once. She hadn't meant to sound so shrill. She softened her tone. "I only meant to say you startled me. I didn't know anyone was around here."

"There's a village five miles that way." He pointed. "I'm from there."

"You said that last night," Ruxandra said. "I remember."

"Oh."

"Yes."

Say something to him. Anything. Don't stare at him like a fool. Say something!

But he was the one who spoke first. The words were soft and hesitant. "How did you come to be here?"

"I—" She tried to think of how to explain it. *The truth is always the best answer. Just not the whole truth.* "My father was killed, and I was . . ."

Turned into a monster? Made a creature of darkness who craves blood?

"Violated."

"Oh." He turned away. "I'm sorry."

"I ran and found a village." *Why didn't I stay there? Think.* "The men there attacked me."

"What?" The boy's head came up, and his eyes went wide. "How could they do such a thing?"

"I—I was alone. They thought they could take advantage. So I ran again."

He went silent and scuffed his boot some more.

What if he thinks I'm impure?

"I forgot!" He jumped to his feet, a look of dismay on his face. "My mother always said I was a fool with no manners."

He stepped back, took a deep breath, and bowed. It wasn't a very good bow and certainly not a courtly bow, but it *was* a bow. "My name is Neculai Lupei. My mother is Oana Lupei, and my father was Petre Lupei. I am most pleased to make your acquaintance."

Ruxandra rose and gave her best formal curtsy—the one the nuns made her practice for hours. "A great pleasure to meet you Neculai Lupei. My name is Ruxandra—"

What do I tell him?

"And my family name is one I would prefer to keep secret. So you may call me Ruxandra."

"I see." He sounded unsure, but nodded and smiled anyway. "Then please, call me Neculai."

For no reason she could think of, Ruxandra started giggling. She clapped her hand over her mouth, but that didn't stop it. Neculai's head cocked to one side as he watched her try to contain her laughter, which only made her laugh even more. *He'll think I'm terrible!*

Then he laughed as well, and everything was good again.

When they both managed to stop, he smiled. "It is all very odd, isn't it?"

Ruxandra nodded. "Yes. It is."

"Can I ask where you came from?"

"I do not know." *Now I sound like a fool.* "I mean, I do not know where it is from here. I was raised at Our Lady of the Mountains Convent. Near Bucharest."

"That is a long way to come." Neculai rubbed his chin. "How did you get here?"

"Walking, mostly," Ruxandra said. He was still standing, looking down at her. She scooted over on the log. "Please, join me."

"Thank you." His long legs stretched out on the ground in front of him. He kept his distance—not so far as to seem unfriendly, but not so close as to seem presumptuous. Ruxandra liked it a great deal.

His brow furrowed. "You walked here? In winter?"

"Yes." It was the truth, and Adela always said it was best to lie using the truth. That way you didn't have to remember anything. "It was cold for a great deal of it. I had lost my boots and cloak. And I hadn't been able to bathe for weeks before you saw me."

"You should have come to our village," he said. "Everyone would have helped you."

"I . . . cannot. I do not like villages. Not after what happened."

She hoped her tone sounded sad enough that he would leave the matter alone. He nodded and didn't pursue the subject. "How did you survive the winter?"

"Hunting," Ruxandra said. "I'm a good hunter."

"You are?" He sounded surprised. "I didn't think they would teach hunting in the convent."

Ruxandra laughed—it wasn't that funny, but she felt like it was something she should laugh at, so she did. "No, I learned hunting along the way."

"Do you need food?" he asked. "Because I have a loaf of bread I would be happy to share."

"Thank you, I'm fine." Ruxandra shifted her gaze to the sky. The stars were bright, and the dawn was a long way off. She could stay talking all night if she wanted to.

And there is no Sister Sofia to ruin things, either.

Neculai looked up and sighed. "It is very late, isn't it? Do you have a place to stay?"

"Yes! I do!" The words flew out of Ruxandra's mouth. *I cannot have him know I'm hiding in the woods like a beast.*

No, not like a beast, like a hermit.

But I still don't want him to know.

He rose and offered her his hand. "Then would you like me to walk you back?"

She took his hand. His skin was warm, and his pulse moved through his fingertips. It made her stomach buzz and her head feel light. She was so close to him. All she had to do was step forward and embrace him. It was a strange thought. She'd never embraced a man before. Yet all she needed to do was take that single step.

She squeezed his fingers. "Thank you but no. I would . . . I need to get to know you better," she said, "before I show you where I live."

"Of course." Neculai blushed again. "Stupid of me. You don't know me at all, and you do not know if you can trust me. Here."

He held out the lamp. Ruxandra stared in surprise.

"You can take it," he said. "I'll find my way home. It's not far, and I know these woods like the back of my hand."

Ruxandra continued to stare at the lamp. A new heat blossomed in her that had nothing to do with the warmth of the light.

She took the ring of it from his hands. Their fingers touched, which made her realize she hadn't let go of his fingers on the other hand. She abruptly did and stepped back. The back of her leg hit the log. She started and wobbled but managed to not fall over. "Thank you."

Neculai smiled. "May I see you tomorrow?"

"Please," said Ruxandra. "In the evening. After sunset. I'll try to get here earlier."

"Thank you."

He bowed once more, then walked into the woods, whistling. Ruxandra watched him until he was out of sight. Then she turned and headed back to her den, skipping with each step.

"He likes me. I can tell he likes me. We're going to be friends. I know it. And then perhaps . . ."

Perhaps what? It's not like you can stay with him.

"Shut up," she hissed. "I know I cannot stay with him. I don't want to stay with him. I just want a friend."

But it's not just a friend you want, is it?

"Shut up."

She awoke early the next night and raced out as soon as the sun was below the horizon. She found one of the fawns and drank it down, then dropped its body and ran again. Instead of going to the pond, she went upstream and found a place where the clear, small brook ran over stones. She splashed herself again and again until she was sure all the blood was gone. Then she dashed back to her den and got dressed. It was still light when she reached the pond.

He sat on the log, waiting.

The butterflies danced in Ruxandra's stomach, but they had become familiar and made her smile. She walked around the pond. He rose and bowed to her. "Ruxandra. Welcome."

She giggled and curtsied. "Neculai. Thank you."

"Now that you're here, we can get this lit."

He stepped aside, and Ruxandra saw a small fire pit dug into the earth. He knelt beside it. "It was very nice talking to you in the dark last night, but I thought—"

Blushing, he busied himself with his flint. Ruxandra sat on the log—close but not close enough to touch—and smiled. "You thought what?"

He didn't look up, though his blush deepened. A spark from his flint caught the small handful of tinder, and he blew on it until it became a little flame, then laid it under the little stacked cabin of logs. He blew some more as the fire caught the smaller kindling. He sat back, seeming pleased with himself.

Ruxandra waited until she looked at him to ask again, "You thought what?"

Neculai swallowed hard, and the blush came back full strength. He stared at his shoes. Finally he sat straight and looked her in the eye. "I thought I would like to be able to see your face tonight."

Now it was Ruxandra's turn to look away, though she was smiling as she did. *How sweet.* "That would be very nice. Seeing your face better, I mean."

He smiled. "Good."

"So . . ." *What does one say to a boy?* "Tell me of your family. And the village. What's the village like?"

He shook his head. "It's not that interesting. It's just a village."

"I spent ten years in a convent," Ruxandra said. "It cannot be less interesting than that."

Neculai laughed. "I doubt that. But then again, our village boasts over two hundred souls."

Ruxandra put on a serious face and nodded. "Impressive."

"Oh very." He made his voice as grand as he could. "We have a mill. We have a blacksmith, *and* we have a baker."

Ruxandra clapped in exaggerated delight. "How amazing!"

"There is a proper inn for guests to stay whenever they come to the village."

"That is most exciting."

"It is owned by my uncle."

"How wonderful!"

"You could stay there." All the joking left his voice at the words. His eyes were locked on hers, and he looked very serious. "He would let you stay for free for a little while. Or you could work there. He always needs girls to work in the tavern because they keep getting married. Then you would be close by, and I could see you in the day."

"No!" Ruxandra shouted the word.

Neculai's face fell, and he leaned back. "I'm—I'm sorry."

"I cannot." Ruxandra felt panic rising. "I can't go into a village. Ever again. I will not do it." She pushed herself as far down the log as she could. *I'll get thirsty and everyone will know what I am—a monster.*

"No one is going to make you go into the village." Neculai's voice was calm like Sister Mary's when she was convincing the goats they needed to be milked.

"Good." In an instant she saw it all—her life in the dark of the woods, hunting, then hours with the boy, being almost human.

You're not human.

He reached out and put his hand on hers. "I promise you."

His touch melted all her fear. The feeling of his rough, strong fingers touching the back of her hand drove almost all rational thought from her mind.

"I'm sorry." Ruxandra felt foolish. "I'm sorry. I didn't mean to shout or scare you. I just—I can't."

Neculai squeezed her hand, then let go. He turned to the fire and poked at it with a stick. "Tell me about the convent."

Ruxandra smiled. "Well, there was a goat that liked to climb onto the chapel roof at milking time."

They talked for hours. Ruxandra told him about Adela and Valeria, though not about their intimacy. She had no idea how he would react. She talked of the sisters and Mother Superior and the lessons they had been forced to learn. He told her about the woods and woodcutting and about how his mother had wanted him to learn to read and go into the clergy. She demonstrated the three different curtsies she'd learned as a child—formal, familiar, and royal—and the various ways a young lady was supposed to sit when in the company of others. He taught her an owl call and raven call. She did an impression of the cook that left him gasping with laughter, and he gave his best impression of the miller his sister had married.

The fire sank lower and lower as the night went on until there was nothing but a few red coals glowing in the night.

Neculai yawned, finally, and smiled at her. "It is very late, and I must chop wood in the morning."

Ruxandra stood, and he rose with her. She curtsied the familiar curtsy for friends. "Then I had best let you go."

"I greatly enjoyed this evening," he said. "Will you be back tomorrow?"

"Certainly," Ruxandra said. "Sometime near sunset."

"I hope so," he said with a grin. "So how is a gentleman supposed to say good-bye to a lady then?"

The butterflies, which had been fluttering in her stomach, danced. She hesitated, then extended her hand. "A kiss on the hand is considered genteel."

"In that case . . ." He took her hand in his, bent over, and brushed his lips over her skin. It sent an electric shock through her. He straightened, then smiled. "Was that right?"

She didn't know how she had come to be standing so close to him or how her hands got on his chest. She only knew that her lips were so close to his and that it would be a terrible shame not to kiss them. So she stretched up her mouth to his and brought her lips against his, and for a single, dizzying moment, the butterflies and warmth and electricity raced through her all at the same time.

His body trembled. His pulse pounded as his heart raced. His sudden gasp and the way his hands reached out and caught her waist and how rough his lips were made her want to pull him closer, to feel him in her arms, and to put her mouth on his neck . . .

She made herself step away from him. Then she turned and fled into the woods.

I almost drank him. I wanted to drink him.

CHAPTER
THIRTEEN

THE NEXT EVENING, she ran even faster to find food. She chased down the deer herd, found a fawn, and jumped on it. The little deer started and tried to run. Ruxandra sank her talons into it. It screamed and kicked and squirmed. Ruxandra ignored all that and sank her fangs into its neck. She drank hard and fast, sucking the blood out of the creature until its life faded away. The brightness of its youth was not so surprising anymore. It just felt like food.

Is it enough?

She ran back through the woods. Her plan had been to rinse off and meet him at the pond, but she was scared. The night before had been so lovely. He'd been polite and hadn't tried to make her go with him. It seemed like he liked her, and she definitely liked him. It all seemed to be going well.

Except the part where you almost drank him.

"Shut up." Ruxandra cast her eye through the bushes. She spotted a rabbit hiding in the underbrush. She changed direction and pounced, catching the little ball of fur before it could move. She ripped open its throat and drank it down in a moment.

More. I should have more. More will keep me from hurting him.

"Yes." She dropped to her haunches and sniffed at the air. Squirrels were nearby. They chattered above her. There were deer in the distance, but she didn't have time for more fawns. She needed to eat, fast. She searched around, making sure he was nowhere in sight. Then she jumped.

Straight up she went, so fast that the squirrel didn't have a chance to react before she grabbed it. She tore its throat out on the way down and drank it dry in seconds. She threw the small, furry corpse away, then ran again. She sniffed for prey as she moved through the trees. She found two more rabbits and flushed them out. She nearly tore them apart in her haste to get at the blood and had to drink fast before they died.

I must look awful. She needed to get clean but didn't want to go near the pond in case he was already there. She went to the stream instead, downstream of the pond so no blood would flow into it. She found a two-foot-deep pool and stepped into it. She scrubbed and scoured, soaking her face and body to get all the blood off. Then it was back to her den and the towel. She patted hard to get dry. She dressed, then ran back into the woods.

She was full—more than full, she was stuffed. "Which is good, because I do not want to do anything bad."

Then stay away from him.

"Don't be stupid!" The words came out as an angry whisper. "He's a friend. My only friend, and he is good to me, so shut up shut up shut up!"

There he was.

She stopped on the edge of the woods to straighten out her dress and to watch him. He'd set new logs in the fire pit, ready to be lit as the last of the light faded. He had a bottle with him and a small loaf of bread. To Ruxandra's delight, a set of shepherd's pipes sat to the side.

She stepped out into the open. "You play?"

A smile lit up his face and it made her knees tremble. "Oh good, you came."

"Of course."

"I was worried." He looked away, embarrassed. "I mean, after you kissed me, you ran off so fast I was worried you regretted it."

Ruxandra looked away. It took her a moment to get the words out, and she couldn't meet his eyes. "I do not regret it at all."

"Good." He stood. "Because I didn't regret it either. In fact, I enjoyed it. Very much."

Ruxandra turned, and there he was, right in front of her. She gazed into his brown eyes. He cocked his head to the side. "I've never seen eyes like yours before."

"Really?" Ruxandra didn't think her eyes were any different than his.

"So pale blue. They're almost silver. It's amazing."

"Thank you."

Pale blue? My eyes are brown. My eyes were *brown. They must have changed too.*

"Your nose is very pretty too."

Ruxandra pulled herself from her thoughts. "Is it?"

"It is. But not as pretty as what's beneath it."

Ruxandra managed to keep her eyes on his. "And what do you see beneath my nose that is so pretty?"

"These." He leaned in close, and his lips pressed against hers. Shocks and butterflies raced through her body. Her hands wrapped into the fabric of his shirt, pulling him close. His arms surrounded her in his warmth. She felt her lips parting under his as they had done with Adela and Valeria. She barely managed not to put out her tongue.

I cannot have him think of me as a slattern. He's too nice.

She pulled back and smiled. "When are you going to play for me?"

He stepped away, smiling. "Right after I get the fire started."

She took a spot on the log and watched the fire come to life. When it was burning to his satisfaction, he sat on the log beside her, then raised the pipes to his mouth. He ran his breath up and down the openings a few times, then launched into a quick dance tune. Ruxandra's smile grew even wider, and she began tapping her foot to the dance beat. He smiled back—not an easy trick to do while still playing—and stood. He danced quite well, considering he played the pipes at the same time. He turned and bent with the music, ending on one knee on the other side of the fire.

Ruxandra clapped. "Oh, very well done. Play another!"

He obliged, playing three more tunes, all fast and happy. Ruxandra jumped up on the second one and danced around him while he played. On the third, they danced together. Dancing had been part of the girls' education at the convent—after all, they were to be married and had to entertain. They held hands and went through the steps of a *courante* as best as they could. He finished, bowed, and then began a new tune.

This one wasn't a dance song. The notes from the little pipes soared, sad and sweet, into the forest around them. It was a song of longing, of reaching, and of remembering. The slow, measured meter and the soaring notes dug into Ruxandra's soul. She sat on the log and watched him as he played, never missing a note.

When the song was over and the music faded, Ruxandra put her hands on either side of his face and kissed him. This time she did not restrain her tongue, letting it slip past her lips and onto his. His tongue met hers, and for a time, nothing else mattered.

It would be so easy to kiss his neck.

Ruxandra stopped the kiss and sat back. Neculai's eyes opened. There was a question in them that Ruxandra was sure she couldn't answer. She fluttered her hand like a fan in front of her face and pretended to catch her breath. "I have become a hussy in your eyes, no doubt."

"No!" Neculai's protest was loud. "Not at all. In fact, I consider you to be a lady above all others."

Ruxandra rolled her eyes even as his words warmed her. "A lady doesn't open her mouth so fast when she is kissing. In fact, a lady should never kiss any man except her husband."

Neculai opened his mouth to answer, but Ruxandra put a finger over his lips. "Stop, before you say something you'll regret."

Because you can never be my husband, and I do not want you to say it.

"I could never regret—"

"Oh, stop!" Ruxandra tapped his lips and pulled her hand away. Touching him was exciting her, making it hard for her to think. "My turn. You gave me a concert, so I should give you one."

Neculai's eyebrows went up. Then he nodded and stood. "Excellent. What instrument did you bring?"

"My voice."

"Which is already as sweet as any bird's," Neculai declared. "Sing for me, my lady."

"Flatterer." Ruxandra thought for a moment. Most of the songs she knew were religious. The nuns allowed almost no secular music. *Even so, there must be one . . .*

So she sang a very old song from "Chartivel":

> *"Hath any loved you well, down there,*
> *Summer or winter through?*
> *Down there, have you found any fair*
> *Laid in the grave with you?*
> *Is death's long kiss a richer kiss*
> *Than mine was wont to be—*
> *Or have you gone to some far bliss*
> *And quite forgotten me?*
> *What soft enamoring of sleep*
> *Hath you in some soft way?*
> *What charmed death holdeth you with deep*
> *Strange lure by night and day?*
> *A little space below the grass,*
> *Hour of the sun and shade;*
> *But worlds away from me, alas!*
> *Down there where you are laid."*

Neculai's mouth hung open when she finished. "That was . . ."

When he didn't finish, Ruxandra suggested, "Horrifying? Terrible? Enough to scare the birds from the trees?"

"Beautiful," he said, his voice firm. "Very beautiful. But very sad. Do you know any happy love songs?"

Ruxandra cast about in her memory. There were others, she was sure. Adela used to sing them while they did the laundry or worked in the garden. In fact, there was one.

"Oh how I wish to see my love,
My love so far away.
He says he loves me, yet he goes
On journeys of many a day.
I have not gone with,
For my father raged,
And my mother quailed with fear.
For well they know I would give myself
To the one I love so dear.
So next time that my love goes,
My love so far away
I shall go with him,
And dance with him
And enjoy many a day
And when my father comes after
To drag me from his bed
I shall not go
I shall not go
For we two shall be wed!"

Neculai laughed and applauded. "Beautiful!"

Ruxandra curtsied, sinking low in front of him. "I thank you, kind sir."

He reached out before she could rise, catching her hand and her shoulder and guiding her forward to sit on his lap. "Yet even the most beautiful song cannot be more beautiful than you."

Ruxandra looked away, smiling. "You said that to get kissed again, sir."

Neculai pretended to think a moment. "Did it work?"

As a reply, she pressed her lips to his, and for a brief moment, nothing else mattered. There was only the warm, delicious boy, and it was so much better than with Adela and Valeria, and she was happy.

The hunger stirred.

It was not the desperate need she had felt when she drank the old woman, nor was it the terrible madness that had caused her to kill her father, but it was there, strong and powerful and craving. She found her lips leaving his to kiss his cheek, his forehead, his ear. Then lower, to kiss his neck.

To linger on his neck.

To gently suck at the skin of his neck.

To—

NO!

It took effort this time to pull her lips away. She could feel her mouth shifting, feel the fangs preparing to come out. She sat back and smiled, though she kept her lips together.

He smiled back. "I have not enjoyed anyone's company so much and so well for such a long time."

"I see. How many others' company have you enjoyed?"

She was rewarded with a flush that started at his chest and went all the way up. She caught his chin in her hand. "Tell me their names. All of them."

"All of them?" Neculai's eyes widened until he looked the perfect picture of innocence. "Why do you think there is an 'all'? Perhaps it is just one. Or none."

"Liar." Ruxandra arched a brow. "You are strong and tall and handsome, and if you haven't bedded a full hand of women, I'll be surprised."

"Then be surprised." He grinned back. "Because I have not bedded five women."

"Six then."

"Two."

"And were they pretty?"

"Not as pretty as you."

"Liar." She pulled his hair, giving it the gentlest of tugs. "Tell me the truth."

"They were pretty," he said. "One was the miller's sister, who bedded me to spite the man she loved. He married her. The other—"

Ruxandra broke the silence. "The other?"

"Was Daneila." His voice had changed. The teasing and happiness had vanished. He looked into the fire. "She was lovely. She had blonde hair and brown eyes. I would bed her in her father's fields, and she loved me with all her heart."

He fell silent. Ruxandra felt like an intruder, a thief stealing his memories. "You loved her."

He nodded.

Ruxandra bit her lip. "And then?"

He shrugged. "She died. She cut herself harvesting the wheat. It didn't heal and grew red, and in the end . . ."

Ruxandra wrapped her arms around him again, pulling his head to her breast. "I am so sorry."

He shrugged. "Death is unkind. But it comes to us all."

He might have been trying to make the words casual, but they held so much pain, so much heartbreak that Ruxandra had tears coming to her eyes. She lowered her face to his, kissing him again and again. He didn't respond at first, but as more of her kisses landed on his lips, his arms came tight around her, and his lips pressed hard against her. His hands moved up and down her back, and her fingers tangled in his hair. She wanted so much to comfort him, to make him happy and take away his pain.

Forever. I can take it away forever. The thought jolted her. She pulled her lips away and caught his arms. He froze.

Gently, ever so gently, even though she wanted to throw off his arms and run away deep into the forest, she pushed his arms from her and rose to her feet. She leaned in and kissed him on the forehead. "I must—I must go. Before tonight . . ."

"I understand," he said. His voice was rough with passion and pain. "I do."

"I know." She backed away from the fire, into the darkness. "I will see you tomorrow. I promise."

"I'll be here too."

She backed away until she was in the tree line, then she turned and ran back to her den as hard and as fast as she could.

CHAPTER
FOURTEEN

RUXANDRA TORE OFF THE dress when she reached the den. She hurled it at the bed. The chemise followed a moment later. "I am so, so stupid!"

She kicked the wall, denting it and sending dirt raining down.

"How could I want to drink him? How could I want to hurt him like that?" She kicked the wall again. "I am not a beast. I'm not!" She fell to her knees, tears rolling down her face. "I want him so much."

You want to drink him.

"I want him!" Ruxandra screamed. "I want to be with him! I want to touch him! I crave touching him! What is wrong with me?"

She grabbed her breasts hard as if the pain of her nails digging into the flesh could drive away the desire. But all it did was inflame it. "Oh God, I want him!"

You'll kill him. He'll die. It'll be your fault.

"Shut up!" She squeezed her breasts harder. One hand slipped off, driving down between her legs. Her sex was wet and ready and desperate. She howled in frustration and rammed three fingers inside of herself. It hurt, and it felt good, and she did it again and again until she hit climax, and still, it wasn't enough.

"I want to be with him. I need to be with him!"

Why?

"I don't know!" Her shout shook the dirt from the ceiling of the den and echoed so loud it made her ears hurt. She slapped her face a dozen times, trying to shake off the desire. When that didn't work, she used her fingers again, hitting climax after climax until the sun began to warm the den. She fell back, exhausted and crying. She should have been relieved, should have felt better, but all she could think of was touching him.

Drinking him.

She crawled under the cloak and rolled into a ball. "I just need blood. That's all. More blood so I can be with him. So I will not hurt him. And I will get as much as it takes. I swear I will. I just need more blood."

There's the village nearby.

"No." The word came out as a whisper. "No, I can't."

Why not? You've done it before.

"No, no, no, no, no!" Ruxandra turned her face to the wall. "It's his village. I cannot kill people he knows."

So you're fine with killing people he doesn't know?

"No!" She pulled the cloak tighter around her. "I do not need to kill people. I can control myself. I'm not a beast. I'm not a beast."

She pulled the cloak over her head and muttered the words again and again.

She dreamed of the angel. The touch of a fingertip to a fang, the silver blood that fell onto her tongue—the blossom of pain that was, in the dream, no longer pain but a terrible pleasure, a gateway to life and power. She felt herself grow bigger, more understanding of life and death, though there were no words to describe what she understood—the idea was too big for words. When she awoke, it was gone. But there had been something . . .

When night fell, she slipped out of the den. The sky above was dark gray, and the smell of moisture filled the air. Ruxandra closed her eyes and sniffed, searching for a smell past the threat of rain.

She retraced her steps from the day before to the small grove where she'd found the fawn. She sniffed harder at the air. There were no fawns nearby, but there was larger prey. For a moment she was afraid. She'd never killed anything so large. But the hunger was driving her.

A doe came into sight.

She dropped to a crouch, and her talons came out. She circled it, getting upwind of it and staying as silent as possible. Her fangs slipped down into her mouth, ready to bite and rend.

"More blood," she whispered so quietly that not even the deer's sensitive ears could hear her.

It wasn't a young deer or a small one. It was a fully grown doe, as large as she, with long legs ending in powerful hooves that could break bones if they hit and powerful teeth that could tear her flesh apart.

Ruxandra didn't care.

She crept closer to the beast, hoping it wouldn't see or smell her. A deer's first instinct was always to run, and Ruxandra didn't want to chase it down. She wanted to catch it fast, drink it down and go back to the stream. She would wash herself off and get dressed and see him again, and it would be fine, because she wasn't going to be hungry at all.

A twig cracked beneath one of her feet.

The deer took off like a bolt shot from a crossbow. Ruxandra snarled and leapt after it. It dodged in and out of the trees, raced across any open ground it found, and slipped through the bracken and underbrush like it wasn't there. Ruxandra raced after, bouncing off the trees and tearing her flesh on the underbrush. The deer broke into a clearing and took off at a mad sprint, racing faster than Ruxandra imagined possible.

It wasn't fast enough.

Ruxandra caught up to it halfway across the clearing and leapt, trying to sink her claws into the doe's back. It whirled at the last second, and she went over. She landed on her feet, skidded and leapt again. This time, the doe was ready, up on its hind legs. It smashed out with hooves, hitting Ruxandra in the face and sending her backward. She hit the ground hard, landing on her back. The deer took the moment to turn and run, but Ruxandra was already up and springing once more. This time she got a claw into the beast and dug deep into its flesh. It let out a scream of pain and whirled again, hooves flashing.

Ruxandra dodged and leapt a third time. Her claws dug into the doe's chest, and she shoved her mouth forward, latching onto its neck. Her teeth ripped in deep, and the deer's big vein exploded with a gush of blood. As much spurted out onto Ruxandra and the ground around her as got into her mouth. The deer kept struggling, throwing itself forward and back and trying to drag Ruxandra against the ground to get her off. She kept clinging, kept drinking.

The doe's motions grew more and more feeble until it could do no more than lie there gasping. Ruxandra kept drinking, even though her stomach swelled from all the blood. When the last of the deer's life faded away, she let it go and stood.

She had never felt so full before.

She staggered her first few steps then righted herself. "I'm not hungry anymore. I won't be hungry tonight. At all."

She stumbled into the forest, picking up her pace as she ran. The deer blood turned sticky and hard as it dried. "I'll need to stop at the den and get the soap."

She looked at the sky. It had grown darker and not just from the setting sun. The clouds grew thick and heavy and in the distance, rumbling thunder. "I better not be so late that I miss him. Not tonight."

She picked up her speed, moving faster than the growing wind. She got back to her den, retrieved the towel and the soap and then went to her deep spot in the stream. Getting the blood off seemed to take forever, and getting dry took even longer.

It was dark by the time she reached the pond. She was clean and smelled of lavender. Her hair was still wet from the bath but was untangled and free. She had on the dress and chemise and regretted not bringing the cloak. Water spat from the sky, large drops smacking hard against the leaves. The wind grew more ferocious with every second.

Neculai stood by the pond, holding a lantern and turning in circles, looking. The water of the pond rippled and shook, a miniature ocean, rolling in the oncoming storm. As soon as she saw him, she ran straight to him. "Neculai! You shouldn't be out here!"

"Neither should you!" He yelled to be heard above the roaring of the wind. "It's going to be a bad one."

"My place is shielded enough."

"So is mine." He grinned. "But I didn't want to be there without knowing you were safe."

"Well, I am."

"And so am I." He looked up. "And we are about to get very, very wet."

As if his words were their cue, the clouds opened up and dumped their burden of rain. Neculai grabbed her hand. "Come! Quickly!"

Ruxandra let herself be pulled through the whipping branches and down the path. The rain sloped sideways with the wind, denying them the cover of the leaves and plastering their clothes to their skin. The lantern went out before they were halfway down the path. Neculai kept running, his feet swift and sure on the path until they broke free of the dark forest to the clearing around his hut. He didn't let go of her hand until he had pushed the door open and pulled her inside, out of the rain.

He slammed the door shut against the wind and turned the bolt.

"Wait a moment." He reached onto a small shelf holding a tinderbox and a flint. "I'll get the fire started."

Of course, he cannot see. "Get dry first. Otherwise, you won't be able to light it."

"Don't worry. I've done this before."

Steel sparked against flint three times, then four, and on the fifth caught. He blew on the tinder and lowered it into the fire pit. The kindling was already stacked, as neatly as it had been by the pond. Ruxandra watched him squat beside the pit and get the fire going without dripping water on it. It was very impressive given how small a space they were in.

When the kindling was crackling and the fire was licking at the bigger logs, he stood and looked at her. Then he laughed. He covered his mouth but couldn't stop. "Oh my, you are soaked."

Ruxandra looked down. Her dress was plastered to her body and was dripping enough to leave puddles on the floor. He was no better, his clothes soaked and stuck to his skin, his hair matted down over his forehead and sending trickles of water down his face.

She laughed too. "So are you."

"We can't stay like this," he said. "We'll catch our deaths."

The butterflies flew back into Ruxandra's stomach with a vengeance. "Then . . . what do you suggest?"

He blushed and cast his eyes around the room. "Right. I have two blankets and my spare cloak. You get the cloak, I'll use one of the blankets, and we'll use the other one as a towel. I promise to keep my back turned until you're changed."

She wanted to say he didn't need to turn around, that he could help her undress, but it was too forward. She nodded instead. "Thank you."

He thrust the cloak at her and reached past her to get the blanket. As she took the cloak, her hand brushed his, making her stomach flutter all the harder. He smiled at her—a quick, nervous grin—and stepped to the other side of the fire pit. He put the blanket on the table and began peeling off his shirt. The wet fabric clung to him at first, then gave way. Ruxandra watched as the shirt slid up, revealing the strong, thick muscles of his back.

She desperately wanted to undress.

The fastenings on the dress were hard to get undone, and the sleeves stuck to her body. She was acutely aware that he was only a few feet away, and she was stripping away her clothes. Her hands shook, making the ties on the dress even harder to undo. She got them free and let the dress slip down. It fell to the floor in a sodden lump.

Her chemise was soaked through too. It clung to her, showing off every inch of her body. She struggled to pull it over her head without tearing the fabric apart as she had with her old dress. *Had it only been a few days ago?*

Then she was naked, and the cool air in the cabin slipped across her skin, raising goose bumps and making her nipples hard. She grabbed at the blanket and rubbed at her flesh until she was something close to dry. Then she picked up the cloak and slipped it around her body.

Ruxandra took a deep breath to steady herself and gripped the cloak shut. She turned around and saw that he had wrapped the other blanket around his waist, leaving his back bare. She swallowed hard. "I'm—I'm done. Did you want to dry off?"

"Yes, please." He turned and reached for the blanket they were using as a towel.

His bare arms and chest were strong and muscular and glistened with water. His skin was light brown, his nipples much darker. They were hard, like hers, from the cool of the room. There was little hair on his chest, though a small trail of it ran from his navel downward, disappearing beneath the blanket.

Ruxandra wrenched her eyes up and shoved the blanket forward. "Here!"

He took it and began drying the water from his chest and arms. Ruxandra watched. He turned and began rubbing the towel across his back.

"I can do that for you!" The words were out of Ruxandra's mouth before she could stop them. "If you like, I mean."

He looked over his shoulder, his brown eyes piercing into hers. There was nervousness there and anticipation and desire. His smile was more tentative than before. "I would like that, yes."

She stepped forward and took the blanket from his hands. She placed it on his back and with gentle, easy circles stroked away the water. He sighed as her hands rubbed tenderly over his skin. She found herself coming closer and closer until there were only inches separating her flesh from his. She breathed deep, and his scent filled her head. It was muskier than before, like an animal in rutting season. It was enough to make her drop the blanket, though her hands didn't stop moving on his skin. She leaned closer and closer, then kissed his bare shoulder.

Rainwater. Sweat. Flesh. The salt tang. The—

Neculai turned around. His arms went around her waist, drawing her tight to him. The cloak slipped open, and she felt the bare skin of her belly touching his and the rough wool of his blanket pressing against her. He leaned in and kissed her, long and slow and gentle. She kissed back and their tongues played together. His fingertips ran down her back, going lower than they had before. He cupped the curves of her backside and used them to pull her even tighter to his body.

For the first time, she became aware of his sex. It was pressed against her belly, long and hard, like the men in Adela's pictures. *Though not that long. Valeria was right.*

Ruxandra ran her hands up his chest and down his arms, up his arms and down his chest and his belly to where the wool blanket formed a dividing line between innocence and desire. She knew she should stop, knew a lady would step away, but she wanted to touch him so badly.

She let one hand slip past the border of the blanket and rub the length of him. Silky. Hot. He groaned with pleasure. She caressed him again then stepped back. His eyes were wide with passion and desire. She continued backing away, continued moving until her legs touched the bed. The cloak was open, right down the center. Her breasts were half-hidden, but he could see her belly, see the hair between her legs. His eyes lingered there. She felt her sex liquefy, melted by the warmth of his gaze.

She didn't care about being a lady anymore.

His eyes flicked back up to hers. Her lips parted at what she saw there.

She reached up and pulled the cloak off her shoulders, feeling every breath of the cool air moving over her skin, outlining her body.

Neculai moaned with pleasure. He fell to his knees in front of her and wrapped his arms around her waist. He kissed her breasts, caressing the pale nipples with his lips and his tongue until they became harder than ever before. He rose, and their mouths met again. His heart raced. His face and chest were flushed red. His breath came in short, hard gasps between kisses.

The blanket fell from his waist to the floor.

Ruxandra ran her hands over his bare backside, over the sides of his thighs. She reached between his legs and touched him, feeling the hardness and the softness of his length. His pulse beat through it in a strong, steady rhythm. She glanced at it. It was large, and it was her first time, but she wasn't scared. She wanted it. She kissed him and fell back and pulled him close.

"Please," she whispered. "Now. Please."

His chest pressed against hers as he reached down with one hand. She felt his heartbeat through his chest, felt the blood racing through his veins as he caressed her, making her cry out. She felt his sex pushing against hers. Then he moved his hips forward, and she gasped, and then his pulse beat inside her.

There was no pain. Nothing had ever felt so good.

It wasn't only the pleasure. It was the closeness. She'd been so lonely. He was not only with her but *in* her, and she gave him pleasure too.

This was what people—lovers—did, night after night. The thought filled her with a golden fire, like the sunlight she once enjoyed. Like the first mild, sweet May morning of the year.

She pulled him tight to her, wrapped her legs around his waist. She gasped in rhythm with his thrusts. It was as if they were one being. *Everything is right.* She had to kiss his lips, had to kiss his cheek and his hair and his ear. *This is what lovers do.*

She *needed* to kiss his neck and feel his heart pounding.

Oh God.

Needed to put her lips against his flesh so she could feel his blood racing.

God, no.

Needed to sink her teeth into his flesh and drink and drink and drink.

No!

And then her teeth tore through the flesh of his neck and he started screaming.

H E BUCKED AND THRASHED as he screamed. His hips rammed hard against her in a grotesque parody of his gentle movements only moments before. Ruxandra's claws sank deep into the flesh of his back. Her legs wrapped tight around his waist. Her mouth was clamped on his neck, and she could not make herself let go.

Please, God. Don't let me kill him. Stop. Stop!

But it didn't matter how loud she screamed in her head. It didn't matter how she strained at her muscles and her joints, how hard she tried to pull her mouth away, or how many tears rolled down her face. She *could not* let go.

His blood—hot and rich and so much better than the doe's blood—poured down her throat. Her mouth sucked harder and harder, trying to get every last bit of it out.

He weakened. His struggles faltered and were easier to contain. His screams faded, becoming small and plaintive, like the cries of an exhausted child.

No. Oh God, no. Please, no.

She tried again to make her body let go, tried to pull her mouth from his neck. Nothing would move. His life started to fade. She could almost see it in her head, as if he were dissolving in front of her.

No!

She reached out with her mind and grabbed hold of him, pulled him to her and wrapped herself around him. His body groaned; his muscles went limp. His heart slowed and stuttered. His body grew heavier. His sex went soft and slipped out of her. But she could still feel his spirit—feel his soul—wrapped in hers. It was like wrapping a new kitten. It struggled and squirmed, wanting to be released. She clung onto it instead, praying with all her heart that she could keep him alive.

Once I stop drinking. Once I have control of myself again. I'll put his soul back into his body.

She didn't know how she would do it. But she knew she had his soul, held inside of her. So she would find a way to save his body, to put him back, and to bring him back to life. Just as the angel did to her.

And then what?

He will not forgive me. He won't let me come near him ever again.

But he'll be alive.

He stopped breathing, and Ruxandra had control over herself again.

She shoved his limp body off hers. It bounced on the side of the bed then slid to the floor. One arm fell into the fire pit, where the flames licked at his hand. Ruxandra grabbed him and pulled him up onto the bed. He seemed to weigh nothing, and he practically flew through the air. His head hit the wall.

"I'm sorry," Ruxandra whispered. "I'm sorry, I'm sorry, I'm sorry. But you're here with me, right? You're still here. So go back. Go back to your body."

She closed her eyes. His soul was terrified. It wanted out, to be free. She pushed at it with her mind, trying to send it back where it came from. Terror rose as he realized what she wanted. It wouldn't go back to the body, wouldn't budge at all.

"I know you're dead." She put her hands on his still chest. "I know I killed you. But you can go back. Just go back for me. Please. Please, go back."

It wouldn't move.

"Dammit, go back!" The scream came out raw and loud. Inside her head, she shoved as hard as she could, trying to drive the soul out of her and back into its body. The soul's terror was palpable. He tried to grab at her, to hang on, rather than be returned to the corpse.

She screamed again.

And pushed again.

And still, he wouldn't go back to his body.

Because he's dead.

Because I killed him.

Because I'm a beast.

Except she wasn't. Not anymore. She had stopped being a beast the moment his blood started flowing into her throat. The mad desire that had possessed her had vanished. She no longer craved being touched. No longer needed to feel another's company. She had been like a cat in heat, desperate to be filled.

Except it wasn't sex she had wanted, not really. Most of it had been her body's way of drawing her close. What she wanted— what she *needed*—was blood. Human blood. But her mind had been too dulled to realize that. Or too naive. Her animal desires had taken over, coaxing her into proximity, seducing her to touch and to kiss and to let him enter her body, all so that she could drink him dry and kill him.

Surely that wasn't the only reason? She'd been happy, before. But the happiness had slipped from her grasp, like she didn't deserve to remember.

Inside her, his soul squirmed again. He didn't reach for his body though. He didn't reach for anything that Ruxandra could see. But he was reaching. He wanted to be let go, to be set free to continue his journey.

I ought to let him go.

I can't.

Ruxandra cocooned the soul inside her mind, wrapping it in layers of warmth and love and desire. She didn't want to let him go—couldn't let him go. Not after killing him like that. She wanted to be with him to take care of him and protect him. If that meant having to share her mind with him, then she would.

Better than being alone.

She stood up from the bed. Neculai lay like a dropped puppet, his limbs pointing off in different directions, his hands tight claws. She straightened his body first, then his legs. She crossed his arms on his chest and straightened the fingers. She gently turned his head to face the ceiling. He had a gaping hole in his throat, though no blood flowed from it.

Ruxandra fell to her knees, buried her face in the mattress, and screamed.

Ruxandra screamed her helplessness and her rage, her anger and her fear. She screamed at the demon that made her a monster and the body that would not obey her and would not even *die* like it was supposed to. She screamed out her grief at Neculai's death and her anger at herself for killing him.

When she could no longer scream, she wept.

When the last of her tears were gone and she felt nothing but hollow inside, she rose from the bed. She covered Neculai's body with his cloak, kissed his head, and went to the door.

She didn't bother to pick up the dress or the chemise. There was no point pretending she was human any longer. No point in trying to preserve anything of the person she once was. She was a monster, and monsters didn't need clothing.

The moment she opened the door, the wind slammed into her like a living creature, trying to knock her to the ground. The rain pounded against her flesh like ten thousand tiny hammers, each trying to beat her into submission. She closed the door behind her and stumbled down the path. She wended her way through the rough-cut stumps of the trees that Neculai had cut.

I should bury him.

But if I do that, his family will never know what happened. They deserve to know.

She left the clearing and stepped into the slight shelter of the forest. Branches whipped back and forth in the wind. Some struck her in the face. The rain still blew sideways, soaking her from head to foot. It didn't matter to Ruxandra. None of it mattered.

The rain couldn't hurt her. Nor could the cold. She couldn't get sick. She'd probably never die. She'd just go on murdering for all eternity.

Before all this I thought I was going to be a princess, married and raising children.

Then I thought I could become a hermit, dedicated to God. I was going to dedicate my life to God. Instead, I became a beast. An abomination.

I am lost to God forever.

She stepped into the clearing around the pond. The log where they sat was soaking wet, the water streaming off the sides of it and filling up the little fire pit where they had sat together, singing and laughing and talking and kissing.

Ruxandra thought she was crying again, but the rain pounded so hard on her face she couldn't feel her tears. She trudged away from the pond. There was no point in hurrying the rest of the way back to her den. Dawn wasn't going to come for hours yet. She wasn't hungry anymore, and she had nothing to do.

She trudged through the woods, letting the rain soak her and the wind shove her and the branches whip against her. An hour later, when she reached the den, she stood outside it, staring at the hole in the earth that she had been turning into a home.

She lay in the mud outside her door and stared at the clouds. She would stay there until the sun drove her into the den. She opened her mouth and let the rain pour into it. It wouldn't drown her. Wouldn't even choke her. Nothing would kill her.

Perhaps a lightning bolt.

Perhaps.

But the lightning was gone, and all that remained was the water sheeting down on her. She lay still, trying not to think of what she had done and what she was, and failing—*his arms around me, his eyes so warm and lively, his kiss, the blood, his terror*—until she felt the first heat of the sun, burning bright and hard and unforgiving, behind the clouds.

The lantern was the first thing she saw when she stepped inside. She stared at it, remembering how he had given it to her to light her way home and how she had looked at the flame until morning had come. Her eyes went from it to the bed frame and the cloak spread across it. Neculai's scent wafted from it to her, and the tears grew stronger.

She grabbed the cloak and the chemise and the lantern with a single motion. She stepped back out into the rain and bundled the chemise and cloak around the lamp. Then she pitched them together as far out of her sight as she could. They bounced off a tree and landed in the underbrush less than a hundred yards away. Ruxandra turned her back on them and walked back into the den.

She curled up on the empty frame. The knots and breaks in the branches dug into her flesh. She embraced the pain of it and stared at the ceiling of the den until the sun began to rise.

Somewhere around noon, sleep came.

She felt the sun going down but didn't move off the frame. Some of the pointed ends of the branches had dug into her in the night, leaving scrapes and dents in her flesh. She ignored the pain. It was small and almost unnoticeable in comparison to the pain inside her mind.

She wasn't hungry though.

Further proof that animal blood isn't enough.

With the animals, she had to eat every day and eat a lot. With human blood, she was still as full now as she had been when she'd finished murdering Neculai.

She waited until full darkness had descended before leaving the den. She picked a direction away from Neculai's cabin and began walking. The sounds of the woods filled her ears, though she no longer cared. She didn't need to hunt rabbits or anything else. She could walk all night without having to stop, and for the next night. She would get as far away from this place as she could manage.

An hour later, she realized she wasn't alone.

It wasn't a scent that caught her attention but a feeling—a deep-seated knowing that something else was out there. It wasn't a human—she was sure of it. It wasn't an animal either. She sniffed at the air, trying to pick up its scent. It wasn't close enough. But there was something out there, and it followed her.

She stopped walking, closed her eyes, and listened.

A vision leapt into her brain. She was back inside Neculai's cabin, and she was starving. She slammed again and again against the walls, trying to break free. Rage, burning high and bright, filled every inch of her being. She wanted to escape the cabin and feed. She needed to feed.

Ruxandra's eyes flew open. She was alone in the woods. There was nothing near her except the animals.

Only she still felt herself locked in the cabin. She felt the mattress shedding under her ragged claws and jagged teeth. She felt the pain of stepping in the coals of the fire and heard the howling as she jumped away. She hit the door and banged against it. It moved. She slammed against it once, twice, and on the third time, broke through and tumbled out the cabin onto the wet ground.

But I'm not doing that. I'm right here.

Still, she raced through the woods, like another layer of reality had been placed over the world. A thin layer, a veil she saw through into the real world beyond. The more she concentrated on the real world, the fainter the vision became. It never went away though.

What is going on?

Thinking of it brought her back to the vision. In it, she moved through the woods, running fast. She broke into the clearing and to the pond. She went around it, feet spraying mud as they dug into the ground. She ran harder. Ruxandra recognized the route she took.

She headed for the den.

Why?

Why am I seeing this?

Fear, sudden, sharp, and overwhelming, filled her, bringing pain to her stomach and new tears to her eyes. Within her, Neculai's soul struggled, desperate to escape.

She didn't know what she was afraid of. All she knew was that something very, very angry was coming and she needed to get away from it.

She turned and ran. She tore through the underbrush and dodged trees. She wanted to run full out but couldn't. The vision overlay everything, making it harder for her to see where she was going. She was reduced to near-human speeds as she tried to keep her balance.

In the vision, she chased herself. Through the eyes of the vision, she saw herself go into the den. She inhaled her own scent and the trail she had left. She then loped through the woods, hard on her own trail.

This isn't possible. I'm right here. Right here!

Ruxandra kept running until the sky brightened. She cast around for a hole—any hole—that she could crawl into. She looked for a depression in the land, an overhang, anything at all. The sky kept growing brighter. There was nothing in sight. Her fear of whatever followed her began to slip away, replaced by the sure, terrifying knowledge of what would happen when the sun touched her.

I do not want to wake up in a grave. Not again.

At last she spotted a tree that had been uprooted in the wind, tearing open the earth beneath it. She dove into the space under the roots, digging frantically, widening and deepening the hole. Ruxandra tunneled like a badger, desperate for a place that would protect her from the sun, pushing and shoving and throwing dirt until she had a place hidden from the light where no direct sun could reach. She heaved a sigh of relief.

Then the vision returned. She was running through the forest, charging at full speed over the very ground she had traveled. Ruxandra pushed herself farther back into the hole. The sun was rising, the heat of it came and the terrible light that would burn her to a crisp. In her vision she ran faster and faster, over the hills, through the woods, heading like an arrow toward her hiding spot.

It cannot be me. It can't. I'm right here.

A new scent filled her nose. It wasn't human, though it had been. The aroma of dead flesh, sweet and sickly with the beginnings of decay, came closer.

There was a howl as Neculai dove into the hole on top of her. His hands grabbed at her throat, he screamed, and for one moment she caught a glimpse of a face filled with animal rage, its eyes empty.

Then he collapsed, dead, into her arms.

CHAPTER
SIXTEEN

RUXANDRA SHOVED AT NECULAI's body until she was out from underneath it. There wasn't any space for him in the hole. She managed to get out from under him, but he was still close enough that his dead flesh touched hers. She shuddered and pushed herself as far away as she could.

He smelled wrong. He didn't smell like Neculai anymore. He smelled like death and decay. He was covered in dirt, as if he had fallen a dozen times running through the forest. His skin was gray and saggy on his bones. The hole in his throat was gone, but he was covered with deep scrapes and scratches as if he had ripped at his own skin.

His fingernails were long and thick and sharp and misshapen, as if an uncoordinated child had tried to duplicate her talons by molding them out of flesh and bone. His hands were bent in claws, still trying to grab, though he lay still.

Like they had been when he died.

Worse—much, much worse—were his teeth.

The straight, strong white teeth were gone. In their place, his mouth was filled with jagged, broken, crooked fangs unlike the long, clean two that Ruxandra had. They stuck out well past his lips, and the sharp edges of them had ripped his lips open in a dozen places.

What did I do to him?

The thought was terrible. She didn't want anyone to have her curse. She couldn't imagine making someone become like her. And he *wasn't* like her. He was a grotesque imitation, a twisted broken *thing* that had once been the body of her lover.

It had to have been me. There was no way it could have been anything else. She shuddered, remembering the others she had bitten. Did the same happen to them? To her father's advisors? To the woman in the manor? Did everyone she bite turn into a raving monster? For how long? Was it only for one night?

Because the body that lay before her was dead. There was no heartbeat, no breath. There was no sign of life.

My father's advisors. I saw them the next night. They were still dead. So it isn't everyone.

Why is it him?

She reached inside herself to the soul that lay there. She felt his fury. He tried to break free and escape, but his struggles were weaker than they had been the night before. As if the longer she held it, the more pliable it became. She sent a silent thought to him to calm down, and he did. She suggested again that he go back into his body. He raged and tore at the cocoon surrounding him, frantic to go a different direction. He didn't want to go back into the travesty of life that lay before her.

The soul wanted to leave, to flee this world and not come back.

I'm not ready to lose him yet.

Except I haven't lost him. I've made him into a monster like me.

She scrunched herself back against the dirt. She thought about pushing the corpse out of the hole, but that would mean risking the sun and she couldn't do it. She had to stay next to it for the length of the day. Then she could shove it out of the hole and get out herself. *Then* she would go and leave the cursed creature behind.

But what if it follows? Shouldn't I wait? Take care of it?

She shook her head. *It cannot. It's dead.*

But it was dead before.

She stared at the thing that had been Neculai. Its muscles were too relaxed, its face too slack. There was no life in it. Even so, it repulsed her in a way that the dead had not. When she had first killed him, it had been horrible, staring at his body. Worse than it had been with that woman she'd drank in the manor house. Much worse, because it was Neculai, her lover. But there had been no revulsion. Just anger and grief.

That *thing* repulsed her.

She spent the whole day staring at it, ashamed of her repulsion when it was she who had made it what it was. *Perhaps it just needs to learn.*

She couldn't sleep. And when she at last sensed the sun was out of sight, she squirmed out of the hole, trying to touch the thing as little as possible. She was filthy again. The dirt had been wet with the rain, and she was covered with mud. She ran her fingers through her hair, trying to pull away the worst of it. Then she let it alone.

It doesn't matter what I look like anymore. No one's going to see me ever again.

This is the second day since I drank him.

She wasn't hungry yet, which was a blessing. She could spend the night moving instead of hunting for food. She could get herself farther away from people and find a place where she could live off game instead. Once she dealt with him.

But how do I deal with him? Do I bury him?

A deep, angry growl came from the hole.

The hair on the back of Ruxandra's neck stood on end. She didn't want to turn around, didn't want to see what was going to come out from under the tree. She had a mental vision of darkness and a feeling of fury. There was the scrabble of nails on dirt and the sight of the open air and—

Neculai howled. Ruxandra snapped back into her own mind as he charged out of the hole, his claws reaching, his hands extended to rip into her flesh. Ruxandra let out a yelp and jumped out of the way. The leap sent her thirty feet, hard into the trunk of a tree. She fell gracelessly to the ground, and Neculai leapt after her. She scrambled to her feet and jumped again. She went right over him and ended balanced on the trunk of a fallen tree.

"Neculai!" Ruxandra shouted his name as loud as she could. "Neculai! It's me!"

Neculai didn't respond. He came on fast and strong again. Ruxandra jumped away and spun in the air. She landed in an animal crouch, facing him and ready to strike out with her claws.

"Stop it, Neculai." She raised a hand and extended her talons. "I do not want to hurt you!"

Neculai stopped. His fangs were still bared, his claws still poised to rip and tear. He snarled and hissed. Then he turned and ran. Ruxandra watched him go. She sensed his anger and even greater than that, his hunger. She knew she should go after him, but she couldn't. Her feet felt rooted to the ground. Her legs were wobbling. The look in Neculai's eyes had been one of pure hatred. *Mindless* hatred. There had been no consciousness behind it.

Neculai isn't there anymore. She reached for the cocooned soul inside her. *Because he's here.*

Is that what did it? She had not tried to hold on to any of the others. She had been too insane when she'd killed her father and his men, and it hadn't occurred to her when she'd killed the old lady. It had only been because she wanted to keep Neculai by her that she'd tried to hang on at all. *I still want him near me. But that thing isn't him.*

She sank to the ground and put her hands over her head. The vision came back as soon as she closed her eyes. She saw the world through his eyes. He ran back the way they had come. He moved far faster than a human could. Nowhere near what Ruxandra could do, but it was still very, very fast. She opened her eyes again, and the vision faded away to the background. She sighed and wrapped her hands in her hair, pulling until it hurt.

Am I going to spend the rest of my life seeing him in visions?

She stared at the sky, watching the thin clouds scudding past and the stars beyond them. She could spend all night looking but not every night. She couldn't distract herself. She had to stop the visions from coming.

I must stop him.

But not tonight. Tonight I just want to be still.

She put him in the back of her thoughts, focusing instead on hearing the noises of the night animals and the breeze through the trees. She watched the stars and the clouds and the way the branches moved back and forth with the wind. The more she focused outside herself, the less she felt his presence.

Six hours later, she realized where he was headed.

He was already past her old den, running at full speed down the little path to the cabin. He knew exactly where he was going, she realized. She sensed his intentions and his hunger.

He hadn't fed since waking. He needed blood, like she had. Given a chance, he would take human blood above any other.

Then why did he come after me first? I'm not human. Unless the smell of my blood attracts him even more.

Or his hatred is stronger than his hunger.

Both were possibilities, but neither mattered, because Neculai ran past his cabin and out toward the main road—the one leading to his town.

I cannot allow him to start feeding on people.

I will not allow him.

Ruxandra took off running, moving far quicker than he had. It would still be two hours at least before she caught him. But she knew which way she had come. She could get back before he found his way to the town.

At least she hoped so.

The woods went by in a blur. She weaved in and out of the trees faster than any deer had ever moved. Miles vanished under her feet in minutes. She didn't hit a single branch along the way. She jumped the underbrush when it was too thick to run through. At one point, she left the ground, jumping from branch to branch to get through the thickest part of the forest.

It was an hour before sunrise when she reached her den. Ten minutes later, she was on the road to the village. She breathed deep, trying to catch the scent of dead flesh and rot that had become Neculai's scent.

A woman nearby screamed, loud and long. Ruxandra raced down the road toward the sound. It was a small house on the edge of the town. The door had been bashed open and lay splintered and ruined on the floor inside.

It wasn't a large house—three rooms if including the ladder going upstairs to the attic. The place was complete chaos. The big table that had once stood in the center of the room had been overturned. One of the chairs lay broken and splintered against the wall. Another lay half in, half out of the fireplace. Mugs and bowls lay smashed all around the room.

A middle-aged woman lay on the floor in a circle of blood and guts. Her face had been shredded with claws, leaving one eyeball hanging out of the ruins of the socket. The other was gone. Her dress had been shredded, exposing gouged, bloody pendulous breasts. Her stomach had been ripped open by claws, and her guts spread around the room. Her throat was torn out, and a spray of blood lay all around her.

Ruxandra took in all of it in less than a second.

Another scream—higher and younger—came from the loft above.

Ruxandra reached the center of the room in two steps and jumped. She hit the roof beam above the loft with both hands, found her target while in the air, and pushed off the beam toward it.

Neculai was covered in blood and held a young girl by the arm. His nails had torn rents through her chemise, leaving her almost naked. She screamed and struggled, but she couldn't stop him. He opened his great fanged mouth wide and pulled her toward him.

"Stop it!" Ruxandra's voice rang through the room, loud enough to shake insects from the thatch roof above. She hit the floor beside Neculai, her talons ready to tear into his face.

Except that he had already dropped the girl.

He obeys me?

"Step back from her," Ruxandra growled.

Neculai snarled at her and didn't move.

"Now!"

He stepped back from the girl. Then he turned to the small window. Before Ruxandra could stop him, he smashed through the shutters and jumped. Ruxandra snarled and grabbed the girl. Then she, too, jumped through the window and let the little girl go as soon as they landed. The girl's legs gave out, and she fell in a heap.

"Go to a neighbor's house," Ruxandra said. "Quickly. Do not go back inside."

Ruxandra turned and ran after Neculai. He was headed to the village at high speed, but Ruxandra was quicker. She caught him in less than a hundred yards, tackling him to the ground. He struggled and fought, scoring at her skin with his nails.

"Enough!" she screamed. "Stop!"

He obeyed.

"Do not run away. Get up and return with me to the den. Now."

He stood and waited, still snarling. She got to her feet a second later. He watched as she started backing way, then began following. She turned, then ran, moving slowly enough that he could follow. To the east, the sky lightened. It wouldn't be long before the sun came out. Not long after, the villagers would come looking for them.

They must not find me. I don't want to kill any of them.

But if they're coming . . .

She slowed, her body ready to fight and feed. She grabbed hold of her will and moved. *No.*

Neculai kept pace, his face filled with rage, eyes wide. Snarls escaped his lips every few seconds. But he stayed with her all the way back to the den.

She ducked inside first, and he followed. She pointed at the bed. "Sit."

He sat. She watched him, waiting for him to attack. He didn't. He blinked, and a look of panic came over his face. He reached out to her, and for a brief second, Ruxandra thought she saw a spark of intelligence—of recognition even—in his eyes.

Then he toppled over and was dead.

Ruxandra slumped against the side of the den. They were a good five miles from the pond, farther from the village. The chances of them being found were slim, but there was still a chance. And if the villagers managed to drag them out into the sunlight, she did not know what her body would do to keep her alive..

Murder them all, most likely.

She sat on the floor. The earth and stones were rough and gouged her skin. She ignored them and stared at Neculai's corpse on the bed.

What will I do with him when he awakens?

He obeyed her, and that was something. She could take him deep into the woods and make him live off animal blood like she did. It would probably keep him satisfied.

I hope anyway.

She stayed awake the entire day, watching out the door for any signs of the villagers. No one came. When night fell, she stepped outside and sniffed the air. There was no scent of humans nearby. Nor could she hear any sound other than the usual ones—the sough of wind, the rustle of leaves, rabbits moving in the underbrush.

She caught two rabbits without losing sight of the den. She drained the first, then brought the second back. Inside, Neculai growled and snarled. Then he stumbled out the door.

She held the rabbit out to him. "Drink this."

He snarled at her and shook like an animal, readying to fight.

"Drink it!" She shoved the rabbit at his face. He opened his mouth and sank his teeth through its body. Then he gagged and spluttered and spat the beast to the side. He hacked and spat and gagged again and again. And between each bout, he glared at her with hatred so strong it made her dizzy. She sighed and sank to her haunches, remembering him alive—his boldness, his shyness, his kisses. His blood.

And now there was only hatred.

What am I supposed to do?

Kill him again?

It was a terrible thought. But looking at him—at the monster he'd become, that she'd made—it made the most sense. He sniffed the ground and started to circle the den. His eyes stayed on her the entire time. And every time she blinked, he edged closer.

Tears filled her eyes. She tried to speak and couldn't. She swallowed and tried again. She managed a whisper this time, but it was enough. "Come here."

His eyes glowed. He came close, snarling and drooling. She swallowed again and managed to say, "Stand still and do not fight me."

Back at the convent, Sister Andrea had been in charge of the geese. She would feed them, care for them and, when the time came, kill them. She never used an axe or any other weapon. Instead, she would grab the goose's neck and twist as hard as she could. There would be a cracking sound, and the goose would flap for a few seconds. Then it would be dead, and the novices would pluck it.

Ruxandra had hated plucking them.

She stepped close to Neculai and reached out with both hands. He stayed still while she put them on either side of his head. His hair, once so soft, was coarse. Even the shape of his skull felt different, though she couldn't have said how. She looked him in the eyes. Nothing human stared back at her. Full of dread, she whispered, "I am so, so sorry."

He snarled at her.

Then she twisted his head back so he was looking at his own spine. The crack was much louder than it had been with the geese. He convulsed and fell into her arms, his head flopping onto her shoulders.

She fell with him, wrapping her arms tight around his body. She wept again.

This time I'll bury him. He will not come back. Not after that.
Unless it's not his body bringing him back.

The realization was horrifying and made perfect sense. As long as she had his soul trapped, his body could not die. She had to release him. Otherwise—

The thought came too late.

Neculai's neck popped and crunched, and his teeth sank deep into Ruxandra's throat.

SEVENTEEN

RUXANDRA SCREAMED in pain.

Neculai's teeth dug deep into her neck, ripping open the vein. Blood poured into his mouth as Ruxandra grabbed at his head, trying to pull him off. His grip was strong and tight. He sucked the blood out of her as hard as she had sucked it out of him.

In desperation, Ruxandra slammed him against the nearest tree. His ribs crunched and broke, but still he wouldn't let go. She brought out her talons and rammed them down hard from above. His cheek ripped open, and one eye burst as her claws found purchase in his face. She pulled with all her might, and he ripped away from her, taking flesh and muscle and silver blood with him. She kicked hard at him, and he flew against another tree, his spine snapping as he wrapped around the trunk.

Then she fell to the ground, all her strength gone. Neculai's soul took the opportunity to break out of her grip. She tried to hold it—she couldn't have said why except that it was all she had—but she didn't have enough energy. The soul bounded free of her and flew.

She felt it vanish from the world and started to cry. *If I don't have his soul, then he cannot love me. Not even a little bit.*

Neculai's body screamed and convulsed.

The sound was more human than any he had made since he changed. Arms and legs flung out and spasmed so hard that Ruxandra was sure they would snap.

Instead, his flesh changed.

It had been gray and pasty and loose before, an image of fresh death, still moving. Now it was tight and white and firm. His ragged fingernails sank back into his flesh and were replaced by silver talons that grew long and sharp from the tips of his fingers. His eyes rolled back into his head. His spine, bent and twisted from the impact, snapped and popped itself back together. His broken ribs slid back into their proper places.

Oh God.

Then he rose from the ground. He stayed crouched over, like an ape. His head swung back and forth, and he sniffed the air.

When he opened his eyes, they were pale blue.

There was nothing behind them.

He doesn't have a soul.

Ruxandra's covered her mouth with both hands as if blocking her screams could change what had happened.

Neculai roared, his mouth opening wide. Fangs, as strong and as large as Ruxandra's, filled his mouth. He snarled like an animal, yet much louder and much, much more powerful.

"Stop!" she shouted. "You must stop and you must stay back!"

He didn't obey.

He still doesn't have a soul. It's gone.

Neculai moved as fast as she did, and Ruxandra was unprepared for it. His claws slashed open her abdomen and breasts, and his teeth buried themselves in her face. She screamed and slashed back, tearing holes in his back, sending silver blood spurting. He jumped off her, his wounds healing as he landed.

He spat and coughed, sending her blood spewing to the ground. He howled at her again, then he took off running.

He can't drink my blood. Not anymore. But he still wants to feed. He needs to feed on human blood. Just like I did. He'll drink until he's full.

Will he know when he's full? He couldn't think, as near as Ruxandra could tell. He was an unreasoning killing machine. *What if he cannot tell? What if he kills until there's no one left?*

She wanted to run. More than anything, she wanted to run as far away as she could and never look back. She wanted to disappear into the forest. She could live off animal blood and hide from all humans. That was the easiest thing.

I'm responsible for everyone that creature kills.

I've made things so much worse.

Everything she tried to do made things worse—either for herself or for others. Every time she came near people, she hurt them. She had found someone she might love, and she'd killed him. And she had unleashed a monster even more terrifying than herself.

She remembered the feel of Neculai's flesh against hers, his warmth and his wonderful smell. She remembered his hopeful smile and his kisses and the way he held her, wanting to protect her, to care for her.

Neculai didn't deserve to be this thing.

I must stop him. Even if it kills me. Perhaps then God will grant me absolution for what I have become.

Perhaps Neculai will forgive me.

She rose on shaking, unsteady legs, still feeling weak from blood loss. She forced her legs to walk, then into a stumbling run. She soon had them moving at top speed. Neculai was far ahead of her. He was outpacing her, his longer legs eating up the ground faster than hers. Ruxandra sobbed and tried to run faster.

He left fresh prints in the mud by the pond. She followed them down the path to Neculai's cabin.

The door had been torn off its hinges. The inside was a mess of destruction from the night Neculai had fought his way out. The place smelled of many people, not just Neculai.

She ran past it and down the path to the village.

She found the first corpses by the road. A young man and woman, their clothes askew. They looked as if they had been about to start making love when Neculai found them. Their throats were torn open. Blood had sprayed in a circle around each.

Then a dozen voices erupted in screams of horror and fear, and Ruxandra ran toward them.

They came from the inn on the edge of the road. People poured out of it like rats from a burning granary. Inside, there were shrieks and the sounds of metal and wood striking flesh. As she ran forward, one of the voices was cut off, replaced by gurgling. Ruxandra shoved past those outside and ran in.

Neculai was draining a big man wearing an apron. A stout woman stabbed at him again and again with a long-bladed knife, but Neculai didn't stop. Ruxandra charged, smashing into him as hard as she could, sending him flying. The big man in the apron fell lifeless to the floor. Ruxandra jumped over him and slammed into Neculai again. Her claws flashed out, scoring hits on his chest and face. He screamed at her and began slashing with his own claws, tearing away her flesh. Ruxandra tried to ignore the pain, but it hurt so much. Neculai didn't seem to care about his own wounds or even feel them. In desperation, Ruxandra shoved her face at his neck and tore into his throat.

Silver blood filled her mouth. It burned like acid. She yanked her head back and spat. The taste, acrid and vile, stayed in her mouth, but she didn't have time to do anything about it. Neculai grabbed both her arms and slammed her against the wall, then against the floor. Then he jumped on her again and again, smashing through ribs while he raked down at her with his claws over and over. She tried to fight back, but the onslaught was too much. He opened up her face, opened up her belly. She twisted onto her stomach and his feet came down hard on her spine. She heard a *crack*, and she couldn't feel her legs. He jumped again and landed on her neck. The *crack* was louder than the first, and she couldn't move at all. The next time he landed on her head.

Everything went black.

When she opened her eyes again, he was gone. The dead man was on the floor in front of her. The woman lay against the fireplace, her neck at an odd angle. She was still breathing.

Ruxandra's lower spine crunched and shifted, though she couldn't feel it. Then something twisted in her neck, and agony shot through her entire body. She could move again, but every twitch hurt. She pushed against the floor with her hands and managed to sit. There were more screams and shouts and the sounds of fighting. Above it all, Neculai snarled and howled. Ruxandra slid her feet under her then staggered upright. She managed three steps, then fell. She was in so much pain.

"Please," the woman on the floor whispered. "Help me."

"Please…"

Ruxandra crawled to her. The woman's neck was broken, and from her shallow breathing, Ruxandra guessed she had broken ribs as well. She wouldn't live through the night.

Which made it easier.

"I'm sorry," whispered Ruxandra before she sank her fangs into the woman's neck.

The woman couldn't struggle. She was broken. All she could do was gasp until her life faded away.

When Ruxandra stood, she was healed.

She climbed to her feet then went out into the street. Neculai was out of sight but still in the town. She could hear his snarls mixing with the screams of the men and women he attacked. She ran straight toward the noise.

Neculai was surrounded when she reached the main square. Seven men with spears and swords moved in a circle around him, thrusting and stabbing. He slashed through one of the spears. Then he spun, faster than the men could ever move, and jumped. One man screamed as Neculai's teeth sank into his throat. The other men descended on him, stabbing and hacking into him with their blades. He dropped the first man as the man's blood spray into the air. He swung out with claws, and another man fell to the ground, howling.

Ruxandra let out a scream of her own, forcing all her fear and anger into it. The noise rang through the square, louder than the screams of the dying. She sprinted forward, catching Neculai in the middle of his own howl. She hit him hard, smashing him against a wall. His howl turned to a yelp of pain. She slashed with her claws, opening up one of his arms. It started healing at once, but it got his attention. He swiped at her, but she was already jumping back.

She slammed the pointed fingers of one hand into his chest, the talons tearing through flesh and bone far more easier than the men's swords. She raked down the side of his body with her other hand, then back up the center.

His testicles ripped free, and his penis shredded. Letting out a true scream of agony, he convulsed. He shoved her away and jumped over the building, leaving a spray of silver blood behind. Ruxandra followed. Neculai landed hard and charged forward, going through the open door of a smithy. A woman screamed. Ruxandra hit the ground and followed. Neculai was drinking from the throat of a young woman. Ruxandra hit him from behind, knocking his victim free.

She got her claws into his back and hurled him down, following him to the ground. They rolled back and forth across the floor, slashing and hacking at one another's flesh. They bit each other again and again, ignoring the vile taste and burning acid of the blood. Ruxandra's world narrowed until all she saw was Neculai. Somewhere the woman screamed and another, deeper voice shouted, but Ruxandra didn't care. All her attention was on the slashing claws and snapping teeth in front of her.

Then something sharp pierced her side.

It *hurt*. More than any of Neculai's slashes, more than any injury she'd had since becoming what she was. She felt the thin length of the blade deep in her side and a hissing sound. She caught a glimpse of a large man, his hand wrapped in thick leather, raising the blade for a second thrust. The iron had been red-hot when it entered her flesh. Now it smoked and hissed, the red fading to steel gray. Then Neculai was on the man, ripping into his throat and drinking for all he was worth.

Ruxandra pressed a hand against her side. The wound had been cauterized by the knife's heat. She rolled on her back, writhing in pain. The wound should have started healing.

Only it didn't.

She watched Neculai drink down the big man, watched the knife hit the ground as it fell from the man's hand. Neculai dropped the man, grabbed the woman, and began drinking her too.

The wound still didn't heal.

Neculai threw the woman down and ran out of the smithy.

Ruxandra, gasping with the pain, crawled across the floor toward the knife. It was just a blade, with a long, smooth tang that would go into the handle when it was finished. It was still smoking hot. Her silver blood coated it top to bottom.

As she watched, the hot metal absorbed all her blood, creating whorls and swirls of silver inside the metal itself.

She reached out a finger and touched it. It wasn't hot anymore.

How come it hurt me?

The whorls of silver—of her blood—looked almost like they were moving. Before she could think through what she was doing, she pushed the tip of the blade into her hand. Blood welled up. She waited for the wound to heal. It didn't.

Did whatever the demon put in me go into the blade when it went inside me? Is that why I still hurt?

Will it hurt Neculai as well?

She sat up, then used the wall of the smithy to brace herself while she stood. When she was sure her legs would hold her, she stumbled outside toward the screaming.

CHAPTER
EIGHTEEN

WALKING HURT SO much.
With each movement, the wound in her side tore. Every step sent a nauseating wave of pain through her body. Tears rolled down her face. She wanted to hide in her den until it healed.

If it ever heals.

A door to a house down the street exploded open, and Neculai jumped into the street.

His face dripped with blood. His hair was matted with it. A dead child—perhaps six or seven years old—dangled from one of his hands. He looked around and sniffed the air. He threw the child hard at the door of the house across the street. The small skull cracked, and the limbs twisted with the impact. Then Neculai jumped after it, slamming himself into the door. Blood spattered off his body as he hit, and when he jumped back, there was a bloody imprint of his shoulder on the door.

"Girl! Get away from there!"

Ruxandra turned. Behind her, a dozen men with spears lined up, their faces white with fear and grim with determination. They readied to charge at him.

They'll all die.

She couldn't allow it.

She turned her back on the men then staggered forward. It hurt, but she kept going, forcing herself to move faster with every step. By the time she was halfway to him, she was running. When she was three-quarters of the way, she moved faster than any human could.

He broke through the door.

"Neculai!" Ruxandra screamed, knowing there was nothing left of him in that creature. It was his body, but he wasn't there. That didn't matter though. All she had to do was get his attention.

It worked.

He turned and snarled at her, and she drove the dull blade forward with both hands, right into one of his eyes.

He jerked backward, screaming louder than he'd ever done. He fell to the ground, his hands clapped over the gaping hole where his eye had been. He writhed in the dirt and howled in agony.

Ruxandra fell on him like the vengeance of God.

Her hands moved in a blur of speed as she stabbed his chest again and again. He brought his arms down, trying to protect himself. She drove the knife into his other eye, sending blood spraying and making him thrash even harder. His screams and howls grew louder until she managed to pierce his throat. After that, there was nothing but gurgling.

"Die!" Ruxandra screamed at him. "Die! Die! Die! *Why won't you die?*"

Still, he kept fighting, even as his silver blood sprayed all around him.

Ruxandra shoved the dull blade into his shoulder joint. She twisted it and wrenched it back and forth until the tendons snapped and the joint separated. She grabbed the limb and ripped it the rest of the way from his body. He thrashed even harder and tried to bite at her. She shoved the talons of one hand through the bloody sockets where his eyes had been, pinning his head to the ground. She drove the blade into his neck with the other hand and began sawing. Around her, the men formed a circle, their spears pointing at the pair of them. No one came close though.

Neculai's bones cracked and broke, his spinal cord severing with a snap. The last of the tendons gave way, and Neculai's head came off in Ruxandra's hand.

And still it kept snapping at her.

She dashed it mouth-first against the ground a dozen times. The teeth snapped, and the jaw broke. She tossed it aside and went to work on the rest of the body, hacking off the other arm, then both his legs. It was awful, bloody work. Silver ichor sprayed over her flesh.

When she finished with the legs, she stood.

The men around her still had their spears pointed toward her. She turned in a slow circle, taking them in. Their eyes were wide with fear and horror. Several looked ready to flee, others ready to vomit. Their knuckles were white around their spears.

She remembered that she was naked save for the coating of blood—both silver and red. She didn't have it within her to care. One of the men swallowed and took a step forward. He was very unsure of himself. His eyes shifted from her to the spear and back again.

He's going to attack me.

"I am Princess Ruxandra Dracula, daughter of Vlad Dracula, *voivode* of Wallachia. Put down your weapon."

"You are not!" The words were blurted out of another man in the circle. "The princess went missing when her father was murdered. She's dead."

"Yes," Ruxandra said. "I am dead. And I am still her."

The men went pale. Several prayed. One dropped his spear and stumbled away.

Ruxandra looked at the head. The broken jaw still moved, trying to bite. She picked it up. "Where is the town square?"

The man who had stepped forward first pointed. "That—that way."

"Pick up the rest of him." She walked forward. The pain in her side was worse than before. Fresh silver blood oozed down her side. She still wanted to fall down and cry but knew she couldn't. Not yet.

The one who had spoken fell in beside her, though he kept his distance. "What are you doing?"

"He needs to be left in the sun," Ruxandra said. "But you cannot let the pieces touch. They might join back together, and then he'll come after you all again."

The walk to the town square seemed to take forever. She glanced behind and saw that the men had shoved their spears into the rest of the pieces and carried them as far away from themselves as they could manage. She nodded her approval and kept going. By the time they reached the square, a crowd had formed behind them. The townsfolk kept their distance but followed. Many wept. Some were injured but very few. Most of those who had met Neculai had not survived.

Ruxandra walked to the middle of the square. "Where does the sun hit first?"

The man beside her pointed. "There."

"Give me your spear."

He stared at her, uncertain. Ruxandra grabbed it before he could react and pushed the point of it into the ground between two flagstones, burying it deep enough that it wouldn't fall. Then she took the head and shoved it down onto the raised butt of the spear.

"Put the rest of the pieces on the ground here," she said. "Do not let them touch. When the sun rises, they should burn. If they do not—"

Then what? She had no idea, she realized. "Try putting them in a forge. Or find something hotter. But the sun should do it."

One of the streets from the village square led back to the forest. She turned and started walking away. No one tried to stop her.

There might be time to reach the pond before sunrise.

She made it as far as Neculai's cabin before she collapsed.

The next night, she slid from under the ruins of Neculai's bed. With her remaining strength, she'd crawled underneath it, pulling the blankets over like a tent to cover her from the sun. She had felt the heat of the sun when it shone through the doorway, but it hadn't touched her.

She sat up. The pain in her side was still awful, but not as bad as it had been before. She put her hand on it and felt for fresh blood. None came.

I'm healing.

She still had the knife clenched in her other hand.

She found soap—not the pretty soap he had given her but strong lye soap. She took it to the pond and waded in. The water touched the wound, and she cried at the pain. Slowly, carefully, she washed away the blood and ichor. The soap got into the wound, making her cry harder. She kept at it, scrubbing until her skin and hair were clean.

When she was done, she walked through the woods to the den. The journey took the rest of the night. She stopped on the way to pick up Neculai's cloak. Then she went inside, wrapped it around her, and lay on the bed until night came again.

She could move better the next night. She explored the wound with her hand. It was still open but smaller. She walked slowly through the woods, taking her time, and found a clearing. She sat where she thought the sun would hit first and waited.

She watched the stars all night long. They moved across the sky in a dance as old as the world itself. They twinkled white and yellow and red in a sky that was brilliant shades of blue and purple and black. The stars taunted her with their indifference. She could see the vast wonder of existence, feel the questions in her throat—*Where did it all come from? What is God?*—questions of a human girl with inhuman powers. So strong, possessing nothing. Nothing but death.

When the sun started to rise, she raised the knife to her throat.

One thrust, she thought as she pointed it to the side of her neck. She could feel the pause of her blood beneath the skin. *I thrust in through the vein, pierce my spine, and rip it across. That should make it so I cannot move.*

Then I just have to wait.

Timing was key. She needed to do it just before the sun rose to prevent any chance of recovery. With luck, she'd be burned to a cinder well before her body could move again.

It is strange what passes for luck in this death-in-life of mine.

She watched the light grow, watched the colors of the day come. Peach and lavender and soft, pale green. Gentle colors yet still so brilliant they made her eyes water. Tears of grief spilled down her face—for Neculai, for those she had murdered, and for herself. They were also tears of relief.

A little longer, and this nightmare will be over.

It will hurt. But then it will be done. I will be free.

The sun neared the horizon.

She closed her eyes, breathed deep to take in one last smell of spring—of life—and . . .

Her arms wouldn't move.

Oh please, please, please, let me do this. Please. Let me end it all.

She tried with all her might to drive the knife into her throat. Her arms shook with the effort. The tip of the blade pushed into her skin but would go no farther. She couldn't make her arms move, couldn't break the skin. Her body would not move, would not let her kill herself, no matter what she wanted. Its hunger to survive came as the thoughts of an enemy.

Was there a tiny message threading from one self to another? Gratitude?

No. I do not deserve to live. I'm wrong.

It didn't matter. Her arms dropped to her sides. She looked at the line of fire where the sun would break the horizon.

Then she stood and went looking for shelter before her body ended up in another grave of its own making.

It took three days for her to decide what she must do.

She was walking through the woods when the man saw her. She'd seen him first, of course. She'd just taken down a deer, and the blood filled her belly to the point of bursting. As long as he didn't try to touch her, she knew she wouldn't drink him. So she kept walking.

She'd forgotten she was naked.

He called to her twice before coming over. She tried to walk around him, but he stepped in front of her. Something sharp pricked her belly. She looked down and saw the knife in his hand.

"Lucky me." He leered at her and squeezed her breast. She stared at him as if he were an insect, something nasty that the servants would kill. "A lady as lovely as you doesn't come along every day. I'm going to fuck you front and back, little—"

She stepped into the blacksmith shop just after sunset. The man at the forge looked in surprise at the girl in the ratty cloak tied at the waist with a rope. She had nothing on underneath it, he realized.

Ruxandra held out the knife, tang first. "Can you sharpen this and put a handle on it?"

She reached inside her cloak and came up with a blood-covered purse. "I can pay."

The smith looked unsure. "It will take a day."

"I can wait."

Sister Sofia opened the gatehouse when Ruxandra knocked after sunset. She looked her up and down three times before realizing who she was. Her eyes went wide. "Princess Ruxandra?"

"Yes," Ruxandra said. "Please get Mother Superior."

"Where have you been, girl? It's been months. Everyone thought you were dead!"

"Get Mother Superior."

"I'll do no such thing until you tell me how you—"

Ruxandra pushed the gate open and stepped through. She caught Sister Sofia's robe in her hand and pulled her close. Sister Sofia cried out in surprise at Ruxandra's strength.

"Get Mother Superior," Ruxandra repeated. "Now."

She shoved Sofia hard enough that the nun hit the gatehouse wall.

"Send her to the chapel."

Ruxandra was sitting cross-legged on the floor, staring at the crucifix above the altar, when she heard Mother Superior step inside. The old woman cleared her throat.

Ruxandra didn't tear her eyes away from the crucifix. "Do you think God cares, Mother?"

"What?" The old woman took a few hesitant steps forward.

"I prayed to him so much to help me. To stop me. He never did."

Mother Superior hesitated. "It is hard to believe in our Lord sometimes—"

"I believe in him." Ruxandra stood and faced the woman. "I know he exists. I just do not think he cares."

"It is you," Mother Superior whispered. "Oh, thank God."

"Don't," Ruxandra reached into her cloak and held up her knife. "I need you to keep this."

Mother Superior stared at the knife, then back at Ruxandra. Her mouth moved several times before she managed any words. "What happened to you?"

"A fallen angel turned me into a monster. I cannot be hurt by any normal weapons, and I cannot be killed except by sunlight. I can't even kill myself, and I've tried."

The old woman shook her head. "Ruxandra, what do you mean?"

"I even gave the knife to someone else to have him kill me. I thought if I closed my eyes and held still, just before dawn, he could kill me. I told him what I had done. I closed my eyes, and he went to stab me and . . ." Ruxandra shook her head. "I tore him to pieces. My *body* tore him to pieces, even though I wanted to die."

The old voice quavered. "Ruxandra, what do you mean? You are not a monster. You are . . ."

Ruxandra opened her mouth wide and raised her hands, showing off teeth and talons. Mother Superior gasped and stumbled back. Ruxandra caught her before she could fall, though there was twenty feet between them. The old woman's eyes went wide with shock. Then Ruxandra helped her upright and pressed the knife into her hand. "This can hurt me. Nothing else can. I need you to keep it, in case someone needs to stop me."

"My child—"

"I'm going to go into the woods and stay there. Maybe I'll even die, eventually. Hopefully no one will see me again." She went to the chapel door, then stopped. "Do not tell Adela or Valeria I was here. Do not let them know . . . what I've become."

Then she ran, moving faster than anything else on earth, leaving Mother Superior to gape after her.

I will go to the woods again. I will stay away from people. I will become a beast. I'll forget who I was, what I am, and what I did.

And maybe, just maybe, I'll be able to die.

NINETEEN

T HE BEAST ROSE AND stretched, then padded out of its
cave on talon-tipped hands and feet. The night was dark
and clear and smelled of autumn. The Beast liked autumn,
when the animals were fat, the air was crisp and cool, and the
leaves piled up on the forest floor. The leaves underfoot were soft
and crinkled when it stepped on them.

It couldn't remember how many autumns had passed.

The important thing was that autumn always came, following summer as summer followed spring.

The Beast moved out from its lair in an ever-increasing spiral,
searching for prey. It sniffed the ground and the air but picked
up no game. Food was becoming scarce again. It would move on
soon, to another den farther in the mountains. It was in a valley
with good hunting, even in winter. The Beast had gone there
many times, though it couldn't remember how many.

It caught scent of a deer.

The Beast stood and sniffed the air until it knew where the
creature was. It slipped back down on all fours and moved in an

awkward springing lope, like a misshapen bear. It slipped through the brush and around trees until it reached a tiny clearing. A doe stood under a tree near the edge of it. Its ears were up, and it was scared, but it wasn't moving.

The Beast stared at it and sniffed at the air. Something was wrong. The Beast didn't know what, but something was off. Still, there was a deer and the Beast was hungry. It hadn't had deer for weeks. The Beast crept forward. The deer tried to move but couldn't get up. The Beast moved closer and closer, its eyes darting around the clearing. Something was wrong. The Beast wanted to leave and almost did. But it was hungry.

And what the Beast knew best was that hunger always won.

It sprang and sank its teeth into the doe's neck.

There was a rush of air and sudden movement through the ground. A net, concealed beneath the autumn leaves, sprang up, sending the Beast and the doe into the air.

The Beast screamed and began slashing at the net. A dozen men—humans—leapt out of the bushes. Their bodies were covered with rabbit skins and dirt to conceal their scent. They rushed forward and jabbed at the Beast's arms and legs with long poles topped with thick metal loops. One got around the Beast's foot and pulled. The loop went tight, holding it in place. The Beast pulled at the leg, dragging the human forward. The two on either side dropped their poles and helped the man before he fell. Another loop went around the Beast's neck, then another around one of its hands. One by one, each limb was isolated and held. More men rushed out of the bushes to help hold the Beast in place. Someone blew into a whistle, and more men came. One cut the rope holding the net, and the Beast and the doe tumbled to the earth.

The Beast fought and squirmed and thrashed. The men held it firm and dragged it through the forest. Several times the Beast almost managed to break free, but more men came and held the poles and continued dragging it forward.

They pulled and pushed it into the back of a wagon made of iron, with a large iron cage on it. They closed the door and locked the Beast in. Then they tossed a blanket over the cage and began driving.

Days went by.

The blanket kept the sun's light off the Beast, but not the dreadful heat. It spent its days huddled in a ball, whimpering. The nights it spent hurling itself at the bars. None of them gave way.

Then one night the men threw the blanket off and used the poles again. The Beast ran and fought and jumped around its cage, but the men caught it and dragged it out. They dragged it deep into the earth and tossed it in a stone room with an iron door and left it there in darkness.

The Beast had not eaten in weeks.

There was a noise and light. Men in iron with swords formed in front of the door. A woman dragged a girl down the hallway by her hair. The girl cried and begged as she was dragged in front of the door. She saw the Beast and began screaming. The woman beat her with a riding crop until the girl fell, weeping to the floor. The woman pulled her up by the hair.

The lock on the door clicked. The Beast crouched, ready to spring to freedom. The door opened, and the woman threw the girl into the room. The Beast, starving beyond all reason, pounced on her. Any screams the girl might have made were stopped as the Beast's teeth ripped into her throat. It drank deep and fast, tasting human blood for the first time in more years than it could remember.

When she was done, Ruxandra rose to her feet. Her legs were unsteady, and she felt as if she might pass out. She stared at the woman on the other side of the door. She was tall and dark-haired and looked like a cat ready to lick cream.

Ruxandra struggled to form words. It had been so long since she'd spoken. Her tongue twisting, she managed to say, "Who . . . are . . . you?"

The woman smiled. "I am Countess Elizabeth Bathory. Welcome to Castle Csejte."

Ruxandra shook her head, trying to understand. The world tilted and started to go black. She sank to her knees and looked up at the woman. Her last words before she passed out came out as a whisper:

"What have you done?"

Thank you for reading Princess Dracula!

Dear Reader,

I hope you enjoyed Princess Dracula. It was my honor and pleasure to write for you. Of course I was only relaying the information that my Ruxandra was providing, but I hope I did so with clarity and wonder. Thanks for joining me on this fun and wild ride!

Get ready for many more adventures.

Also, if you're so inclined, I'd love a review of Princess Dracula. Without your support, and feedback my books would be lost under an avalanche of other books. While appreciated, there's only so much praise one can take seriously from family and friends. If you have the time, please visit my author page on both Amazon.com and goodreads.com.

twitter.com/JohnPatKennedy
www.facebook.com/
AuthorJohnPatrickKennedy/
johnpatrickkennedy.net

Made in the USA
Columbia, SC
30 October 2017